Undercover

Barbara Winkes

ISBN: 978-1-7781247-0-9

Cover art © May Dawney Designs

Created with Atticus

For D.

Chapter One

To say I have no friends is not an exaggeration. Those who don't want me dead would like to lock me up. Either one of those things could happen sometime soon, but there's something I need to do first. I made a promise. If I can keep it, there's a good chance I can honor my parents' legacy and keep the business they have given everything to, alive.

It's no small undertaking when every day I'm reminded of what's at stake. I can't be distracted by grief because I'm afraid that time might be running out on me. This is not about me. It's so much bigger than that.

Aside from the more solemn task, I still have a business to run, and I'm on my own just as much as I am when it comes to the secret. This is why at 8:15 p.m., I'm sitting in my office, oblivious to the magnificent sight of the city lights below me.

The Mancini Group encompasses mostly commercial real estate. A part of it is still the industry that gave my great-grandparents a fighting chance when they first made a home here. The cozy restaurant they started out with still exists, but we have several other locations as well. They come in handy in many ways.

The profits are good. I have skilled staff, but I'm not someone who easily trusts. I need to know for myself.

A knock on the door startles me out of my thoughts. Jimmy Bruno walks in, stopping cold when he sees the folders on my desk.

"You're busy?"

"That depends," I say, leaning back in my chair. He knows just enough about my off-the-books mission to be helpful, and I want to keep it that way. Jimmy has been with the organization since he was eighteen, and my dad trusted him a great deal.

Me—I know that he's been working hard to make himself irreplaceable. I can't deny the support he gave me after the incident. I'm not sure that's enough.

If he has anything new to tell me, I'll listen. I may not have friends, but he is one of the few people who have been a constant presence in my life.

"It's late. You've been in here all day. I was wondering if you'd like to come have dinner with me and my parents."

The Brunos are the sweetest people I know, and herein lies the problem. There's been an ongoing misunderstanding, one that Dad unfortunately encouraged. I've known Jimmy for a long time. I know he gets the job done, whatever job it is that needs to be done. I have no reason to question his loyalty, but I'm never going to marry him. I think he knows, though Mr. and Mrs. Bruno haven't quite caught up to the fact yet. It would be cruel to mislead them, or Jimmy.

"I can't. I'm sorry."

"You've got to eat sometime."

There's been talk behind my back regarding the subject. Some say I'm crazy not to go for it—he's handsome, charming, with a knack for business. What no one dares to say out loud is that they've been uneasy since my mother took over after my father's death, with my help and Jimmy's.

The people I deal with on a day-to-day basis are old-fashioned. They'd like to see a "man of the house."

In the 2020s. It's frustrating, not that I can allow myself to get distracted.

"It's kind of you to worry about me, but I'll be fine. Go. I'm sure they're waiting for you with enough food for an army."

He acknowledges that with a smile. "It's likely. That makes me feel even worse. You'll be back tomorrow before everyone else anyway."

"Good night, Jimmy. I'll see you tomorrow."

Knowing that he's lost the argument, he salutes. "As you wish. Good night, Kendall."

I sigh in relief when he's gone, aware that he's not wrong. I'm often the last person to leave the building and arrive when the cleaning crew has barely finished their job. Fortunately, when I needed to step in, I had a business degree to show for in addition to my determination. I had to learn fast. Now, being on top of things is just a matter of comfort as much as it is necessity. My father trusted too many, and it got him killed. Mom tried her hardest, but in the end, it was a broken heart that ended her life. After fifty years of marriage, she held on for another two after we got the call that changed everything.

Now there's no one I can rely on but myself.

It's frightening—and somehow freeing.

I'm the only one left to solve the mystery as I promised my mother—to find out who killed my father.

I might die trying, but I don't think about it all that often.

When I finally leave the office, it's after nine. I nod to the security guard as I exit the building through the back and walk to my car on the illuminated and well secured parking lot. I'm not a big connoisseur of cars, but I also represent the company and the Mancini name. My midnight blue convertible Audi is the perfect compromise between practical and fun...Though there hasn't been much fun in my life lately. I've accepted my obligations. There's no way around them. I can't leave the office early or go on a spontaneous road trip.

All hell could break loose, and that's not an exaggeration.

I drive home, where I quickly shower and change into a different set of clothes, one that wouldn't be appropriate for the office. I bind my hair back into a ponytail and apply only a touch of make-up and perfume. To blend in, not to stand out.

I've had a few theories, right after it happened, and so far, nothing I've learned has me disavowed of those. I might be closer to getting evidence. I've put out the word, cajoled and promised, and someone took the bait. She wasn't at the event on that fateful night, but she knows someone who can get me a guest list.

They may not have pulled the trigger, but someone at that party facilitated the raid that ended in a bloodbath. With that list, I'll be a lot closer to identifying the enemy.

I'll have time to grieve my parents.

I'll also send the message that nothing has changed. The Mancinis still own this town.

It's 9:32. I hate people who are late, unreliable. Perhaps being someone who relies on so few people for a reason, I shouldn't be surprised. It still bothers me as I sit at the counter, sipping my glass of wine. The price is exaggerated, I find. Sure, I can afford it, but I don't see what makes these grapes so special.

The bartender, a cute young blonde fussing over me, is a small silver lining.

"Would you like another one?" she asks, attentive to the fact that my glass is almost empty. "Or can I make you something else?"

"No, thanks." I look her up and down, notice that she's blushing. I don't think she knows who I am, which makes the moment even more satisfying. But that's all it is, a moment. I have no intention, nor can I afford to follow up on it.

Not tonight, anyway, and not while rapid developments are underway.

10: 41. I could have had a lavish dinner at the Brunos', but that always comes with conditions. This place is not known for its excellent cuisine. I'll probably be better off grabbing something on my way back. As I pay for my drink, I leave a big tip, earning me a smile and an even more pronounced blush.

I'll admit it. Sometimes I envy people who can just follow every impulse. That's not the life I chose though.

I'm halfway to the exit when Marina walks in, heading straight for me.

"Kendall Mancini," she says. "It's nice to see you again."

"You're late," I return, irritated that she doesn't even mention it. No apology—she'd better have something good for me.

"Yeah, whatever. I have what you need."

"Are you sure?"

She makes a face as she hands me the memory card.

"Did I ever disappoint you?" She shakes her head, laughing. "No, don't answer that. This was surprisingly tough to come by. You owe me, you know that, right?"

I slide the card into the pocket of my jeans and take out my phone. After a few clicks I tell her, "The transfer is done."

"Great." She leans in and kisses my cheek. "Always good doing business with you. If you need me, you know where to find me. Unless you'd like to stay for another drink...?"

I look around, realizing that the pretty bartender is watching us, her expression pensive.

"No, thanks. I need to head home."

When Marina looks at me, her expression is uncharacteristically somber.

"I hope that whatever you find in there, it gives you peace."

Like she did it for my peace of mind, out of the goodness of her heart, and not for the dollars in her bank account...That's not the world we live in. I'm grateful nonetheless.

"Thank you, Marina. I have to go."

In a hurry now, I barely notice the woman coming in as I head out. It's not a full-on collision, but I jostle her shoulder just a bit.

"I'm so sorry."

"No problem." She smiles, holding my gaze for a few seconds, much like I did with the bartender earlier. It's not the place for a gourmet dinner, though they have a satisfying menu. Other needs can be satisfied if necessary.

I have no trouble setting my needs aside tonight. I have a solid lead.

—ele—

Marina didn't rip me off. The card contains not only a police report, but the list of everyone who attended the party where my father was shot and killed. A private fundraiser featuring prominent names in the business community.

I recognize a few names of CEOs that my parents worked with, that we still work with. A politician who dropped off the scene a while back, obviously eager to keep a low profile. Though the documents allow me to piece together some of what happened that night, the picture is not complete, and it's not for Marina doing sloppy work.

The FBI barged in with a warrant that night, the lights went out, and the shooting started.

I've read reports like this before, and this one is startlingly vague, not just given the implications of the incident. It tells me that either the list isn't complete, or there's a name I haven't been able to put into context yet. A couple of uncles, cousins, I could question them. The business partners brought spouses, maybe adult children. The politician.

Who else?

Did the authorities go out of their way to keep someone off the record? That could only mean one of two things: An undercover cop, or an informant.

If it's the latter, my theory was right.

If it's the former, that would mean...What? Did we all fail to pay attention? I'll have to keep that in mind, but when I see the name Arturo Rossi, I know that I can't have been too far off. His close ties to the Bianco family, and his hate for mine, aren't a secret. I don't see him facilitating a murder, but they would. It wouldn't be the first time.

I get up to stand in front of the picture on my living room shelf, both of my parents younger than I am now, in their wedding picture.

"You can trust me," I say.

The ones responsible for their deaths will be held accountable. I will get it done.

Chapter Two

I am obsessed with Kendall Mancini, have been for some time. She occupies a great deal of my waking hours, and at night, I dream about her.

She doesn't know it, but Kendall is the one who can make or break my career, propel me on the path I want to take, or get me sent to a field office in the middle of nowhere.

The Mancini family is a specific, complicated case. I've been on it, preparing for my assignment for several months.

In the past few weeks, we've been moving up the timeline, because this case turned from complicated to explosive. I don't have a lot of time, but I know I'm ready.

We plan to take down others with her. Kendall is my primary focus.

I'm thinking of her even now as I head out to my parents, a retired FBI agent and a former mayor who have both done their share to keep the city safe, against the rising tide of organized crime. You could say I'm in the family business.

I've seen the results of the machinations and endless feuds from families like the Manicinis and the Biancos, and I'm not distracted by sympathy or the fact that Kendall is a striking woman. She's not a teenager. After running the business first with her mother, and now, by herself, she knows what she signed up for. She knows what's happening on and off the books. She doesn't want or need anyone's sympathy.

I went to the mother's funeral, sat in the last pew as I listened to her rousing speech, about the bond between her parents, their dedication to their family and company, their love story. How Al Mancini's death broke his widow's heart.

How Kendall would work hard every day to make them proud.

No one in the church could take their eyes off her as she spoke, standing straight with her head held high, dressed in black. She didn't use the exact words, but the sentiment came across just as clearly: Whoever pulled the trigger on Mancini senior that night, shouldn't hope for forgiveness.

The official version is that no one knows who exactly is responsible for Mancini's death that night, which is problematic. A ton of evidence was recovered from the room, multiple arrests made. It was supposed to be a quick, clean operation that instead became a war zone, a shoot-out that took Kendall's father. It could have taken mine had he been there, but I was the lucky one. It seems only natural that I accepted a crucial role in making sure something like this never happens again.

———ele———

We, too, value family. My grandmother, my cousin, her husband and two-year-old son, and one of my mom's former aides are present, and it's just a normal Saturday night dinner. Julia isn't just one of most valued employees Mom's campaign ever had, she is also my ex. Our break-up lacked drama the way our relationship did, so everyone, including me, is comfortable having her here.

The conversation I have with my dad in his study is a little less comfortable, but I can't afford to miss the chance. He might be one of my most valuable sources—at the same time, I can't tell him much, and I know he won't like it.

I wait until he pours a cognac for both of us, hands me one glass and sits across from me.

"It's strange how little things change," I start. "One name that often comes across my desk is Mancini."

"I imagine. It's part of the deal in this city." It's a casual conversation, still, but I have to be careful. It's not an easy subject for him.

"Yeah, I got that impression. You met Kendall, I imagine."

"The princess. Yes. Of course, I met her. Is there any particular reason you ask, anything you want to know?"

I don't answer right away, flabbergasted at the unfamiliar tone of his voice. Yes, I've heard that nickname. It's been floating around for a while, but I've heard it mostly from members of the Bianco family, that, or older supervisors.

"Yes and no. I mean there are ways to build a case, but that's usually the small stuff."

"You got anything big going on?"

"Just the usual," I hurry to answer. "She's interesting, to say the least. She and her parents were close."

"Oh yes." This time, there's no reservation. "Honestly I'm surprised at her restraint. There's a time for everything but barging in on that fundraiser was a mistake. Someone tipped them off—we lost some good men that night."

"I'm sorry." As far as I know, he wasn't one of the agents present at the raid, but he had a hand in preparations. Like others, he took his retirement not much later.

"I told them it would be a mistake," he says with an anger that surprises me as it rings still fresh and raw. "I was overruled...Mancini was going to come in. For sure he wasn't going to hand us his business on a silver platter, but he had information. We'll never know what it was. If I read correctly between the lines, the same fires we tried so hard to put out are still burning."

I can't deny it. If there was a power vacuum, the Biancos would want to step in. Kendall Mancini and Jimmy Bruno, Al's right hand man, won't have it, and now she's hell-bent on avenging her parents' deaths. No, the occasional tax evasion isn't our biggest problem here.

I don't want to end family dinner on such a dire note.

"They can't burn forever. What's your impression of Bruno? You think he and Kendall are more than criminal business partners?"

Dad gives this some thought, swirling the cognac around in its glass before he answers.

"If that's the case, it would surprise me. Alphonso liked him, Angela and Kendall, I'm not sure. There was talk about a brief fling. That's all I know."

"Thank you, Dad. That's very helpful."

He sighs. "I'm not supposed to ask."

"No." There's no point in denying it.

"I can't tell you how to do your job, and you know that Mom and I couldn't be prouder of you..."

"But...?" I prompt.

"No but. Be careful."

"I always am."

⁓

We've discussed the various options for making first contact—a business offer, a visit to one of the gourmet restaurants, a side business of the Mancini group and a nod to their humble beginnings, a more private setting.

My persona includes the right background for all three, though the private one might be the best chance to catch Kendall off guard, enough to get my foot in the door.

I might have a good chance, given that she visits a bar named *Lilac* on a fairly regular basis. This is where I am tonight, in a van parked outside, waiting for her.

The demands of running a criminal enterprise have caught up with her, especially without the support of her parents. She still comes around every once in a while, and I have it on good authority that she sometimes leaves with a woman.

That could mean many things, and it doesn't have to mean that she isn't in a relationship with Bruno.

But it gives me an opening, something to work with. Kendall has a type. I can deliver. I don't plan on sleeping with her, but if I can be a distraction as well as her new best friend, I'll be in.

The memory of her eulogy is still vivid on my mind. I have read many transcripts, watched enough videos to have a constant representation of her on my mind. I'm fascinated, but I'm also aware that this story needs to come to an end at some point. I'm eager to get started, though that night we are confronted with an unwanted surprise.

The woman entering the bar is Marina Fiori, a familiar figure who has walked a thin line in the past. She's been sharing secrets with the Biancos, the Mancinis, and law enforcement, wherever she sees the biggest advantage. Just a coincidence, or is she meeting with Kendall, assisting her in avenging her parents? I can't wait any longer.

"That's my cue," I tell my partner with whom I've been waiting in the van. "Wish me luck."

We both know luck has little to do with it.

I'm barely in the door when Kendall rushes out, nearly running into me in the process. That's not exactly the first contact I had imagined, but I'll take it.

"I'm so sorry," she apologizes. Kendall after hours is very different from the ruthless businesswoman who never apologizes, I notice. She wears a suit in the office, jeans and a leather jacket with high-heeled boots when going out for a drink—or hunting for information.

"No problem." I hold her gaze to signal my appreciation. She just smiles and walks away as if to say you wouldn't be the first.

Don't worry, Kendall. If I have learned anything in the past few months, it's that it would be a huge mistake to underestimate her.

—eee—

I go in and sit at the bar counter where I order a Gin & Tonic. My alter ego Jessica Byrne has a new favorite bar in town. She's enjoying her signature drink. The next time Kendall comes here, I'll be familiar to the staff, blending in. I still wonder why Marina was here...I wish we could take her in to ask some questions, but it's not illegal to socialize with a Mancini, and this early in the process it would only serve to tip off Kendall and Bruno.

I want to do this as slow and easy as possible, which is enough of a challenge given that Kendall is probably asking some of the same questions.

It's not my job to uncover the past, but the more I'm able to do just that, the better I can figure out how to fit myself into her life to the point she might lean on me, reveal some secrets to me.

Families like hers thrive on firm loyalty. She needs to know that she has mine.

I make a quick call to set up a trace for Marina, just in case.

I come home to my new apartment, the home of Jessica Byrne. The next time we meet, Kendall will remember that name. The place is a few blocks away from the headquarters of the Mancini group, enough to be convenient, not close enough to be suspicious. Sooner or later, she'll check me out. Thanks to the hard work of my colleagues and I, she'll find nothing out of the ordinary.

—⁓—

I can't help smiling when I go back to the bar the next day to find Kendall's car in the parking lot. Even though this is upscale, it's still a bar, and a vehicle like this stands out. She has good insurance, I know that for a fact—though stealing from a Mancini this blatantly would probably not end well for the car thief.

I open the door and walk straight to the counter, like I did yesterday. The bartender is the same too. She works here four nights a week.

"You're back soon," she says. "I'm glad you enjoyed your time here, even if it was brief."

"Your Gin & Tonic was excellent, and after the day I had, I really need another one."

In fact, the day I had wasn't that bad, just a lot of re-reading on the Mancini Group. Accusations of money laundering and tax evasion have been floating around for some time, but also bribery and extortion. Are they guilty of all of it? When it comes to organized crime, you don't get to the top without those means. There's not a chance in hell that Kendall doesn't know what's going on.

"I'm sorry. Coming right up."

"I'll take care of it," someone says behind me, and now I know my evening's looking up. I know that my boss had her doubts when I settled on my approach, to make the meeting look accidental, rather than seek her out for business purposes. She has a lot of experience over me, I get that—but I know my job, and I am experienced when it comes to women like Kendall.

"You don't have to," I say as I turn around. You can't be too quick, too easy. They might go for it, but kick you out the next morning, no second chance.

"But I do. Forgive me for running into you yesterday, but there's something I had to take care of."

Something to do with Marina Fiori?

"Don't worry. I understand."

"So, you'll let me pay for one drink so I can feel better?"

"It looks like I have no choice."

"No, you don't."

I can't say I blame the women who are easily drawn into something quick and temporary. If I didn't know who Kendall Mancini was, more intimately than most people, I might be tempted. I can't forget the threat she sent out, at her mother's funeral of all places. That's only on top of the rest of it.

This is good. Now I need her to stay. I ponder whether it's the right moment to exchange names, a little too long. My cell phone vibrates in the pocket of my skirt.

"Okay, I'll leave you to it."

"No, wait!" This was not at all the way I wanted to sound. The damn phone doesn't stop. I worked too hard for this moment, studying all the details, convincing supervisors that I was the right woman for the job, and that I knew how to do it better than anyone else. "I'm sorry." I finally hit decline call.

Her gaze is amused, but she hasn't left yet.

"This call doesn't have to do with you needing a drink tonight?"

"Oh, no, nothing important. I was just hoping for some decompressing time. Some conversation maybe. My name is Jessica," I say.

"Nice to meet you, Jessica. I'm Kendall."

She makes a subtle sign to the bartender who proceeds to pour a glass of white wine for her. A crisp Pinot Grigio. I've done my homework in many areas.

"I couldn't help overhearing earlier," Kendall says, obviously not in a hurry as she takes a seat on the barstool. "Your bad day. Can I ask?"

"You can, but there's not much anyone can do. It's work. I need to go yell at a few people."

She laughs, a warm, sexy sound that I'm sure has worked on quite a few oblivious women. "Yeah, that works most of the time. What do you do?"

"Right now, I'm wrestling with investors for a project. I'm new in town, and I've just started my interior design business. I'm still trying to get my foot in the door."

"I see. It's not so easy starting out."

"No, it's not. At least I've found a friendly place. I take that as a win."

She nods. "It's discreet. And the drinks are great."

"What about you?"

"I enjoy a good glass of white, but you know that already. I'm mostly in real estate. In addition to the company, my parents ran the family restaurant that my great-grandparents started. It was important to me to keep it alive."

"A restaurant? What kind?"

"Italian. It's called *Catania*. I'd ask you if you've been there, but you said you're new in town, so it's forgivable if you haven't. It's become more of a hangout for the regulars over the years."

"I'll have to try it though. Italian is my go-to comfort food." That's not just Jessica, and I didn't have to practice to be convincing. It always helps when you can blend a bit of your real-life person into your undercover persona.

"Have you been to Italy?" she asks, and I shake my head.

"Me neither. But if you're looking for an authentic experience, let me know. The chef still uses my great-grandmother's recipes."

"That sounds amazing," I say, thinking how much of a cliché it all is. But the crimes committed by her family are no joke. Neither is good authentic Italian food. I like where this is going.

Not too fast, I remind myself. She seems comfortable now, but she's spooked easily.

I'll have to let her take the lead.

Why does that make the heat rise to my face? I'll also have to go slow on this Gin & Tonic.

As time goes by, we make more small talk. She has another drink, I decline, still sipping my first one. I want to be intriguing, not easy. So far, so good.

I'm not fooling myself. This is only one facet of her. I haven't even come close to meeting the angry hurt woman who pledged vengeance in the church that day, and I'll be mindful of her. Nobody's going to invite anyone for a nightcap today. A subtle tug of war has begun.

"I have an early start tomorrow," she says as she takes a business card out of her purse and puts it on the counter. "But call me for that authentic experience, and if you're still having trouble with investors, bring me some numbers. I could take a look."

"You'd do that?" My surprise isn't entirely an act. It's the plan. I just didn't expect it to go so fast.

"Of course. Good night, Jessica. I look forward to seeing you again."

"Good night. And it's Jess."

"Jess," she says and smiles before she walks away.

I pick up the card with the address of the Mancini Group. Sometime soon, we'll get to look into that vault.

Chapter Three

J immy was right. Most of the offices are still dark when I settle behind my desk. I love this time of day, full of possibilities. Reality always catches up with me soon enough, but for a few minutes, I can lean back and consider the big picture. Until it's time to focus.

It's also the time for my first coffee, black, nothing else—except today I bought a pastry with it. This morning, my thoughts are all over the place. I'm not sure what happened last night, with Jessica. I'd be less surprised if I'd asked her to a hotel for a one-night stand, no strings attached. She seemed interested.

Instead, I left her my card, hinted at possibilities, of a date, or a business proposition. Perhaps she caught me in a weak moment. The reality of my situation is starting to sink in, about the information Marina gave me and what it means for us in the long run, the Mancini Group, and the never-ending confrontations with the Biancos. If I find out that one of them is behind my father's death, the next steps are clear. I can't let down the people who have given me everything, who have made me who I am.

They're the reason I am sitting in this top-floor office, go home to a condo with a stunning view every night. They also instilled in me the kind of values that, to my knowledge, are rare with the Biancos. For them, it's all about the power, the influence, no matter who gets thrown under the bus and run over twice.

Dad, and then Mom, ran a tight ship, but never at all costs. They made sure that the most vulnerable ones were protected. It's up to me to continue their legacy. To make a point.

The clearer it becomes, the more I wish I could still be in bed, my arms wrapped around a woman's warm body. Not any woman. Jess. Damn it. I need to snap out of it.

If I see her again, and it's likely after I made a point of giving her my number, I need to put some safeguards in place. So far, nothing about her screams danger, just a woman trying to get her business off the ground. I put a lot of money into a foundation that helps women with exactly that, and I can provide connections, if it turns out that her company is a fit.

But I also need to be careful, especially if I have no choice but go to the Biancos.

Maybe, for a short time, I had this crazy idea that I could be someone else, someone who doesn't have to care about appearances, reputation, legacy. It's not that Jess has this much power. She's merely a metaphor in this, a beautiful illusion.

I can't indulge in them for too long, and besides, they make me feel guilty, like I'm ungrateful for this incredible privilege I've been given.

I have been at work for an hour or so when Jimmy peeks inside my office.

"Bad news?" I ask, getting up when I see his expression. I sent him the list last night, with instructions.

With a shrug, he says, "We're not sure yet. It seems that Arturo Rossi fell off the face of the earth, so we haven't been able to ask him about the list yet."

"Keep looking." I hesitate for a few heartbeats because this is potentially delicate. But Jimmy has stood by my family all these years. Just because I won't marry him, it doesn't mean he'd cross lines, with my private life or anyone involved. He knows there'd be consequences, and he likes where he is too much to take that kind of risk. "Jimmy? I need you to do something else. You'll have to be discreet about it."

"I always am. You know that."

I show him my phone with the website of Jessica's interior design business.

"I just need a quick preliminary check, to make sure she is who she says she is."

"Sure, no problem. Who is she?"

A woman I met in a bar. I almost laugh at the thought of saying it out loud to him. I have no illusions. I have better kept secrets than this, but people in our business are old-fashioned. I might be indulging them a little too much at times, then again, I'm not looking for love or marriage. We agree to not raise the subject.

"A potential candidate for the foundation. I have yet to see."

"I'm on it," he promises. "What if we don't find Rossi?"

"It might be time to have a talk with Tony Bianco." I can see right away that he doesn't like the idea. "If we wait too long, we'll look weak. They knew we'd get that information at some point, and that we wouldn't be sitting on it."

"His name on a list doesn't necessarily mean that he, or Tony, set things in motion. In fact, they've been pretty low-key in the past year."

Tony Bianco and his wife sent flowers to my mother's funeral. Depending on what we learn in the next few weeks, it could mean that they are interested in keeping things calm and quiet. Given the history between our families, it feels more like mockery.

I can't have that.

"Whatever that means. When did you become a diplomat?" That was meant to be a rhetorical question. To my surprise, Jimmy answers it anyway.

"When we lost Alphonso. Look, I know you're good with the business. You've impressed a whole lot of people. I also understand that you made a promise to your mother, but it might be better not to stir things up."

"Stir things up? Two years, and my father's killer hasn't been brought to justice. Because of them, I lost my mother too. None of this bothers you?"

"It does more than bother me," he says. "It makes me sick. Kendall, I made a promise too. To do my best to keep things going...and to make sure you're safe."

It's too early in the day for this macho crap. I know I'm surrounded by it, and I work around it best I can, but coming from Jimmy, this is rich.

"Perhaps you misunderstood something there," I say, keeping my tone as calm and neutral as possible. "Let's invite Arturo's son for a casual dinner, see if we can figure something out. If we can't, I'll reach out to Tony. And get back to me as soon as you have the information on Ms. Byrne."

He's not happy about it, but he'll do what I say. That's a relief.

"Thank you, Jimmy. That's all."

—ell—

To be honest, Rossi's fate wouldn't be much of a concern to me if I didn't need answers from him. Might be that he got nabbed by law enforcement or the Biancos, either one is possible.

It had been another period of relative quiet when Rossi's daughter Sofia married Tony's son Frank. Old-fashioned times, old-fashioned family structures—when it turned out that Frank was an abusive asshole, she had nowhere to go, or so he thought. My parents took in Sofia, earning the wrath of both the Biancos and Arturo. They didn't care.

Pride in doing the right thing runs in our family, and we don't apologize for it. It wouldn't surprise me if

Arturo wanted to go big about proving his loyalty to Tony, after Sofia "disappointed" them.

Come to think of it, I need to see her too. She took a job in our company and launched a brilliant career. She's smart, dedicated, and loyal. After all these years, she still has the air of someone expecting to get hurt, by random strangers or by someone she loves and trusts.

Thinking of Sofia never fails to fuel my anger, and it reminds me of why I get out of bed every morning, of my goals beyond the Mancini name.

Power matters. I'm never giving up any of it, for marriage, or dubious cease-fires.

Jimmy comes back in at the end of the afternoon, placing a USB key on my desk.

"So far so good," he says. "At least where your potential business contact is concerned. Story pans out. She moved into her apartment three months ago, has a small business and is trying to hit up investors. Still struggling a bit though."

That's almost verbatim the story Jess told me. For the first time today, I can feel a bit of tension leaving my body.

"Rossi?"

"No sign of him yet, but we'll keep looking. When do you want me to call his son?"

"Give it another couple of days," I say. "If he doesn't turn up, we'll have dinner at the restaurant on Saturday."

He nods and turns to leave. Jimmy knows that he has already used too many words today and he's trying to make up for it.

I'll swing by *Catania* tonight to make sure everything's in place—for Saturday, and for Friday night.

On a whim, I call Jess. When the call goes to voicemail, I leave her a message.

Hi, it's Kendall. If you're still interested in talking numbers, I'll pick you up Friday at seven. Bring your stats and an appetite. See you soon...I hope.

I am busy for the rest of the evening, so I miss her answer, a simple text message.

Can't wait.

Everything is in motion. I guess that means anything could happen.

Chapter Four

J immy Bruno is stealthy enough as he follows me around all day like I knew he would. It's a good sign. Kendall wouldn't involve him if she didn't think of calling me back. Fair enough, my phone rings while I'm enjoying a latte in a coffee shop near my apartment and working on a design on my laptop.

Jimmy is drinking his Chai Tea at the counter, reading a newspaper.

I keep looking at my laptop screen even though I'm aware that it's Kendall calling. She leaves the message I wanted to hear—everything is on the table, business and potentially, a date. I won't cross lines I don't need to cross. The fact that she is inviting me to a place that means a lot to her is significant. Next step, headquarters?

I'll pick up any proof of crimes along the way, but what's most important is to understand where her mind is at this moment, and to prevent an all-out war between families.

The Biancos are no saints. In recent years, a few members of their family have turned and disappeared courtesy of witness protection, not before giving us some intriguing insights. Whatever sustains wealth and power. Unlike them, the Mancini family has never been involved in local drug trade, though they have kept their cards a lot closer to the vest. No one has been willing to talk, especially after they lost Al Mancini—but they, too have accumulated a lot more wealth than anyone would with a family restaurant and a handful other locations.

Sooner or later, it will be either the financial trail or Kendall's thirst for revenge that will give us a way in. I hope this will happen before anyone gets hurt, but so far, everything is going according to plan. I have to choose an outfit for my visit to *Catania*. I added up some real numbers for my fake business some time ago.

The *Catania* is where it all began for the Mancinis, the family restaurant on which their empire was built. Today, its income is pocket money for the Mancini Group, but each generation holds on to it—for sentimental reasons, sure, and for the occasional backdoor business that can't take place behind the shiny glass doors of headquarters. They have a few other restaurants sprinkled across the state, the *Adria* brand.

Famous chefs cook up gourmet dinners, sometimes for celebrities.

Catania is different.

As seven p.m. rolls around, I must admit that for the first time I'm a bit nervous. Running into Kendall in a lesbian bar? I have home advantage even though I pretended I just moved to town. She has secrets to keep, I don't, not where that subject is concerned. Jess, or Robyn, I'm comfortable.

I expected Bruno to follow me around, check up on me. We prepared for it. We arrived at the more difficult part sooner than expected. Kendall might be lonely, or she needs a bit of a diversion from the fact that she's about to authorize—or commit? —an execution.

We have something in common. We both want to know what happened that night, and it's ironic that it involves our respective fathers, our families' names. We both have something to prove.

Never a bad thing to be able to relate to your target, in order to build rapport.

The driver she sent parks on the curb a minute before seven. I take a look at my mirror image. Underneath the picture of a woman ready for a date, I'm excited. I'm also cautious.

I sit in the backseat and fasten my seatbelt, for an unsettling moment wondering if I got made already, and where this ride is going. The notion vanishes. Kendall is on a mission. She can't afford to be this blatant.

After close to twenty minutes, the vehicle stops in front of a gate. It wasn't always there. After the restaurant and whatever side business was underway, took off, the grandparents built the terrace and hedge around it which allows for more privacy for the guests.

"Right this way, Ma'am," the driver points out the illuminated door at the end of a small walkway, with the sign above it.

"Thank you."

The place is semi-casual, so I chose a dress, and medium-height pumps, for a warm night out. Kendall steps outside to greet me, and I can see the appreciation in her gaze. She, too, is wearing a dress, an outfit different from her power suits at work, or the one she uses when flirting with women at the *Lilac*.

"I'm so glad you could make it." She leans in to kiss my cheek. I'm not sure what to make of the gesture, or the sudden heat rushing to my face, but there's no time to analyze either of them. "Come on in."

I notice that most of the tables are occupied. It looks like a normal Friday night for a successful restaurant, the perfect front, the perfect story.

"Thanks. I brought these," I say, holding up my folder. "And an appetite as you told me."

"Great. We don't do dainty portions here."

There's a man behind the counter, giving us a pensive gaze. Bruno appears from a door behind him, whispering to him.

"Jess?"

"Yes. Sorry. I was just taking it all in. It's a beautiful place."

"Thank you. It holds a lot of memories for my family." She leads me through an arch to a room in the back where occupation is sparser. A man and a woman are sitting at a table enjoying their meal. Kendall points to another one nestled into a nook, the window the same shape as the arch separating the room. With the candle on the table and the view of the garden, it's quite nice.

"My grandparents did some additions because they didn't want to have to turn people away. Let's sit. Would you like a menu or...do you trust me?"

"That's pretty straight-forward," I joke. "We just met...but you're the expert. Yes, I trust you."

"Good. I promise you won't be disappointed."

Kendall must project a certain image. I'm aware of that, though I wonder if the idea of doing business was nothing more than a ruse. If it is, I have to make sure that it remains part of the plan. I won't be making it into headquarters if enjoying pasta at *Catania* is the end of the road.

"About my firm?"

"Let's eat first," she says. "It's been a long week. I'm hungry too." She gets up and reaches out to touch my shoulder. "I'll be right back."

She gives instructions to the waiter who stands at a respectful distance. He nods.

Kendall has barely sat down with me again when he arrives with a bottle of red. I'm not an expert, but I've heard about this one, and I know it's expensive.

There's a different explanation here if Kendall is serious about business, and it will only work in my favor if she thinks I can be beneficial to the family.

Go with the flow. Pick up whatever I can.

The waiter brings the appetizers, antipasti, and baked parmesan. Everything is delicious. With a sip of the Chianti, it's downright heavenly.

"Perhaps we should talk business now, before I disappear into food nirvana," I suggest. "Wow. This might be the best Italian food I ever had."

"That's what people usually say."

"And the host is so modest."

We both laugh, then I push the subject a tiny bit further.

"As I've told you, I'm trying to attract bigger contracts, but all those regulations and licenses are killing me. I wish I had someone who could cut through all of that so I can just do my job."

She listens attentively, nods. "Well, I have to tell you that's wishful thinking when it comes to business. There's no quick way to do any of it."

Except when you're the family's sole heir and it all falls into your lap?

"My parents were eventually able to expand the business, but it took time, and a lot of hard work."

"I'm willing to work hard."

"I know." She refills both of our glasses. "And I know you came prepared. I hope you don't mind I did some inquiries of my own, but I wanted to make sure neither of us is wasting their time. I have contacts to a foundation that helps women in your situation, and I made a couple of calls on your behalf. They'd like to meet you."

My reaction is instant. Strangely enough, with her, my role is easy, the jaw-dropping not an act. I have to beware. She's a step ahead.

"That's amazing, thank you so much! You're a Godsend. I already don't know how to pay you back. Do you, by any chance, need redecorating at home?"

She laughs. "I'm afraid I don't, but I guess I could ask you for a favor sometime. If it all pans out with the foundation. They are really good at supporting women business owners."

"I look forward to meeting them. Thanks again." I raise my glass to clink it against hers a moment before two waiters arrives. They cleared the table earlier and now bring various samples of dishes—pizza, pasta, meat. Kendall is pulling out all the stops.

Perhaps, like everyone else, she needs to live in an illusion for a little while, and she's privileged enough to make it happen, for her, and for me. I haven't missed the implied statement, that it's understood between us I owe her for helping me with my business, and she will come to collect when she sees it fit.

Everything is going according to plan.

"You are welcome," she says. "I have another surprise for you, but first, let's enjoy."

I do, at least until Jimmy comes to the table, his expression grim.

"Kendall, I need to talk to you," he says without preamble.

"I'm sure it can wait until we've finished dinner?"

"I'm afraid it can't. I'm sorry."

It's interesting, to say the least. I wouldn't have expected him to be this obvious, a stark contrast to Kendall's subtle seduction.

Then again, she wasn't very subtle when giving her speech in church. With these two, you can't take anything for granted. The true nature of their relationship is still not entirely clear to me.

What's clear to me is that she's not happy.

"Jess, let me introduce you to the man disturbing our meal, Mr. Jimmy Bruno, my business partner."

"Nice to meet you, Mr. Bruno," I say as if I hadn't noticed him spying on me the other day.

"You too, Ms. Byrne. I'm really sorry, but this is urgent."

"I hope everything's okay?"

"Nothing for you to worry about. Please enjoy your food, and Kendall will be back with you in a few minutes."

Shaking her head in exasperation, she gets up. "I think we should have more wine at the table." Back straight, she follows him. I have to crane my neck a little to see them disappear through the same door Bruno came in earlier.

It could be that there's news regarding Kendall's quest. They might be talking about me.

Or both.

Chapter Five

"**W**hat the hell are you doing?" Once it's just Jimmy and I in the back room, I don't feel the need to hold back. I take one night to have dinner with a beautiful woman, a couple of hours out of my busy life, and he has to barge in on us?

I know, it's not all him. He wouldn't do it if it wasn't necessary. I'm on edge, have been for some time. That's on me.

"I could ask you the same question," Jimmy says as I sit in one of the chairs.

I frown at his tone, thinking his exasperation isn't entirely justified.

"Come on. You checked up on her. She's all right, and a good candidate for the foundation."

"You're sure that's all?"

"Yes, I'm sure none of this is any of your business. I appreciate your contribution, you know that."

He sighs. "It's not about that. I got word that Marina is dead."

"What?" I'm on my feet in an instant. "When?"

"One of my sources with the department told me just now."

I want to curse, but there's no word strong enough to reflect what I'm feeling. Marina took a big risk. I hate that she got caught in the middle. I hate what this means.

"You still can't find Rossi? Are the police looking for him?"

"No to both. Kendall, all I'm saying is you need to be careful. This woman coming out of nowhere, at this time, I'm not sure it's a coincidence."

"You said her story checks out," I remind him. "Did you do a sloppy job?"

"No, I didn't."

"All right then. This has nothing to do with sweet Jess and her design business. In fact, she could be interesting to us in the future."

"To us, or you?" If I didn't know better, I'd think it sounds bitter. Do I know better?

"I need you focused, Jimmy. We go with the plan, get Rossi's son in here tomorrow, and depending on what he tells us, we go to the Biancos. It's even more important now to make a few things clear."

"Whatever you say."

"Jimmy."

He hasn't missed the warning in my tone. "Everything will be ready. I'm sorry about your dinner."

For all that it's worth. I don't have much of an appetite any longer. I'll have to go back to Jess, pretend nothing happened. Before I do that, I punch the wall hard enough to make my knuckles hurt.

I'll make sure Marina's death won't be in vain, that I'll use the information she gave me to its most effect. No tears. I don't have time for that.

———ele———

I take in the woman sitting across from me, Jessica Byrne, who called me a Godsend. I'll admit Jimmy is right to point out she came out of nowhere, being exactly what I need—someone who provides a much-needed time-out, flattery, maybe more. We can't be cautious enough, and I think I am.

I have the power to set her up with the right people and projects, slowly. She'll appreciate it. I need to stop indulging Jimmy and make sure he understands I know what I'm doing.

If he and I need to clear something more between us, so be it. Right after we dig a little deeper regarding Rossi and have that talk with Tony Bianco. He, too, should have no illusions about what I'm capable of.

"I hope it's nothing bad," Jess says, a question more than a statement.

I push aside the worry that she might be fishing for something. She's simply concerned. If I'm not careful, Jimmy is going to make me paranoid.

"Nothing he should have interrupted us for, but he's thorough."

"You've been working together for a long time?"

She's impressed, a little tipsy—and curious.

"My dad hired him right out of college, so I guess I'm stuck with him. But let's not talk about him."

"What do you want to talk about?"

"Why are you here?" I ask, sensing that I startled her. Good. She's been invading my thoughts far too much, and my only defense is to keep her off guard.

"What do you mean? You invited me. It's been amazing so far." She lets a few second tick by. "You're...fascinating."

"I am? I think it's the wine talking."

"In any case, you're helping me. I appreciate that. I've been so busy lately, I barely had time to eat, let alone a luscious meal like this. I love this place. I'll definitely come back."

"For the food."

She smiles. "Among other things, yes, for the food too."

I want to invite her to my condo, but I'm aware that it's early. I have other things to think about, Marina's death, the upcoming conversations, potentially confrontations with Carlo Rossi and Tony Bianco. There's not a lot of time. If the Biancos are behind this, we need to respond somehow. Send a strong message...and if they're the ones who started it all, which is getting more and more likely...Business school did not prepare me for this.

We have coffee and dessert, but Jess senses that I'm antsy.

"I should come back another time for real," she says. "You have something to take care of?" There's no scorn in her voice. I don't know what I want, to be honest. No one knows what's going to happen after this weekend, and it might be too late to start something...On the other hand, she's a distraction for the moment. Being distracted could get me killed.

"I'm really sorry. I'll make it up to you."

"Are you kidding? This is the best meal I've had in ages. You don't owe me an explanation."

"Thank you for saying that. I'll call you."

"I hope you will."

I see her to the door. The driver is waiting on the curb. "He'll drive you home. Again, thanks for coming."

"It was my pleasure." Jess leans in. I'm so very tempted, almost meeting her halfway, before I draw back.

"See you soon."

I head back inside and join Jimmy at the now empty table. He's frowning.

"What?"

"I know these are difficult times," he says in a softer tone. "I am trying to help, but I need to know that you trust me."

"Why would you even doubt that?"

He doesn't answer my question, changes the subject instead.

"All right, Carlo is coming over tomorrow night. We'll see how that goes."

"And Sunday, we'll pay Tony a visit."

To my relief, he's not questioning the fact any longer. Marina's death changes things.

"We might want to prepare for that."

He can be incredibly helpful, but lately I'm getting more and more irritated with him, the vague hints, the subtle criticism. Perhaps I need to remind him that he is not a Mancini.

"Of course, I'll prepare for that, what are you talking about?"

"I didn't mean just Marina, and whatever else is on your mind."

"Just" Marina sounds awfully dismissive of the person who has given us the first real lead, and he makes me sound like this is some last-minute unorganized effort.

"What's going on with you, Jimmy?"

"Nothing," he denies, and after a few seconds... "Okay, you got me. This is not how I imagined it, and probably not how you did either, and for that I'm sorry. We want to show the Biancos strength, there is one problem."

"What would that be?"

"I know that Angela, may she rest in peace, poured her heart and soul into the family, and the business. You do too. But these are old-fashioned guys, and they aren't used to negotiating with women."

Certain that he must be joking, I start laughing.

"Really, that's the point you're making? Wow. Do you know how much I care about Tony's discomfort?"

"It's not just Tony. Uncle Lorenzo, Luca and Claudia all agree."

That is interesting and also infuriating. They all have plenty of opportunity and should come to me first before they consult Jimmy.

"Agree on what? My mother was a powerful woman. Respected. I don't think you were suggesting otherwise?"

"I'm not. Kendall, I need you to understand me here. A lot of parts are in motion, and we must present a united front. If people knew they could rely on...We could do many great things together."

I didn't lie to Jessica when I said it was a long week. I need to choose my words carefully, as I always do...When all I want is to yell at him. In all the time we worked together, when my parents were still alive, and now, he's learned nothing.

"I thought we already were on the same team."

"It's not the same as being part of the family," he says matter-of-factly. "Al hoped it could happen sometime—and to be honest, I still do. I care about you, Kendall."

"You are unbelievable!"

I get to my feet so abruptly the chair scrapes over the tiled floor.

"Don't you dare assume what my father would have wanted. If you thought he didn't care about my opinion, you didn't know him at all. Pity."

"Kendall, wait! I'm telling the truth. He spoke to me about it several times, how we'd continue his legacy."

I've heard enough, sick to my stomach again, even though I barely ate tonight. Someone I relied on lost their life, once again, and Jimmy goes there? We need to have that long talk sometime soon, but I'm too tired and frustrated to pursue it tonight.

"I'm doing that already, and if my own family, or Tony, can't see that, too bad for them. But I expected more from you. Don't screw up tomorrow night."

I don't wait for a reply. I need to put some distance between us before I can talk to him without shouting.

———ele———

It's not just the suggestion...I know about the rumors floating around. This was why I had to show them on the worst day of my life that I wouldn't budge, wouldn't bend. I didn't burst into tears but laid down the law. Like any man would, like the son my parents didn't have.

But Jimmy came at me with this when an hour ago, Jess sat at the same table. Whether it's jealousy, willful ignorance or simply a blind-spot, I can't have any of it. It's so blatantly insulting. I make my decision in a heartbeat, leave the restaurant, and get into my car.

It's a short drive to Jess's apartment, I realize. I could have almost walked, and maybe that would have taken care of the nervous energy I feel.

Something is about to happen...I am still aghast about the blatant disrespect from not only a predictable source, but the very few people in my personal circle.

Old-fashioned. Prejudiced.

This was not the relationship my parents had, or what they wanted for me. I don't need a man to speak for me.

The house is a duplex with two apartments. I ring the bell, and a moment later, Jess opens the door, wearing a tank top and PJ bottoms. Her expression is calm, showing none of the inner turmoil and confusion I'm feeling. She doesn't seem terribly surprised either.

After she closes the door, I step into her personal space. Her eyes widen, and she takes a breath, obviously about to say something.

The words get lost in a heated, passionate kiss. When she pulls me close, her hands firm on my back, I know that any protest is unlikely.

This is so wrong. Even as we rush to undress each other, eager to feel warm, soft skin, I know that this won't be like those few other times, quick, casual sex for stress relief. The kind of thing I can keep contained, under tabs, and I have to. Sure, my family wouldn't send me to a conversion camp—and I don't think anyone would have the audacity to bring up such a thing, because they know I can hit back harder. That doesn't mean I have a lot of leeway there. Jimmy, as much as I hate his interpretation, and the way he never stops for a moment to question it, had a point.

Who can blame me for wanting a fleeting moment when I can forget about it all?

Jess gently directs me towards a moderately sized but cozy bedroom. She steps out of her PJs and pulls the top over her head. She's not wearing a bra. My dress falls to the floor, and a moment later, she's underneath me, breathless, yielding beautifully to my touch. I brush my fingers over hardened nipples, thrilled when her breath catches in her throat. I lean to kiss her again, deeply, my hand wandering down her body and between her thighs. She moans, sensitive to my touch even with the thin layer of fabric. I can feel the heat gather at my core. It's been too long since I slept with somebody I wanted to talk to in the morning. I can fool myself all I want, but it does make a difference. Especially when everything is on the line. I finally draw the fabric aside, not surprised to feel her hot and ready for me.

"I'm sorry the evening ended so abruptly," I whisper. "Let me make it up to you."

"I am not stopping you." She leans back into the pillow, her hips rising to meet my hand. Neither of us has any illusion as to how long this will last. I pull her into my arms, content to feel her racing heartbeat, but Jess, too, is in a hurry. Perhaps it's clear that we only have a small window of time, that our respective obligations don't mix.

Beyond me introducing her to the people from the foundation, that is. I lose all thought of business, completely losing myself in pleasure when her mouth is on me. She barely takes a breath.

I brush a trembling hand over her hair, then let it fall to my side. My eyes are welling up as Jess guides me through a moment of perfect bliss.

It's dangerous to feel invincible.

Chapter Six

W hat have I done? Guilt comes crashing down on me as I sneak out of bed to take a shower. To help me clear my thoughts or something, I'm not sure. This has all been going too fast. I've never been above using what I could with a target. If a bit of flirting helps, what's the harm? I've done it with men, even though I never slept with any of them, and never had the intention or inclination to do so. I've done it with women.

The plan had been to string her along enough to find out where they are on the mission and pick up evidence of criminal activity on the way, whenever possible.

Jessica would be busy with her design business at some point, and Kendall Mancini who could have any woman—or man—she wanted would lose interest.

Right?

Her conscience seems unburdened. Kendall was fast asleep when I went to the bathroom, and she still is when I get some clothes. I dress as quickly and quietly as possible and go into the kitchen to start the coffee. It will take one hell of a lot more to fix this than caffeine, but it's a start.

This is the biggest case of my career.

It might be my last, and not because the main character could snap her fingers and have me killed.

Damn. I've made fun of and voiced my frustration about guys who crossed the line with an attractive criminal. I've seen it happen. I've become one of them.

Thinking back to last night, to what we did, the blood rushes to my face—and I don't blush easily.

"Is there any chance I could get some of that?" she asks, and I jump even though I heard soft footsteps nearing. "Sorry, I didn't mean to startle you."

"It's okay." Suppressing a sigh, I take another cup out of the cabinet. "Would you like something to eat?"

"I'll have to get to the office soon, and get a change of clothes from my condo, but...If you don't mind, yes." So far, not too awkward. "I'm starving. You wore me out."

Here we go.

"You cringed at that," Kendall observes. "I'm sorry. What I mean to say is, yes, I'd like to take the time to have breakfast. But we could go out if you don't have anything in the house."

It's not a bad idea. Create some distance.

"No, that's not a problem. Just sit. Would you like eggs?"

Nothing to see here, just Jessica Byrne cooking breakfast for her lover on a Saturday morning.

I called her a Godsend. Heaven help me now.

I have all the ingredients for an omelet. Making breakfast is surprisingly relaxing, given that I have the head of a crime family sitting at my table. Over the rim of her cup, she gives me a smile.

I realize that there are still questions that my research didn't answer. Kendall has this relationship with Bruno, mostly business, I assume, though some people tell a different story. Ignorance? Wishful thinking? The fact that she sleeps with women is the worst kept secret, but within the context of local organized crime it's mostly a matter of don't ask, don't tell.

This is not her problem, it's mine.

"Thank you for this," she says. "I don't know...There's been a lot going on."

"You don't owe me an explanation."

"Maybe I do." She sighs. "Things have been stressful at work, and Jimmy...He's been a good friend after I lost my parents. He doesn't seem to understand that more is not in the cards." That's quite the post- one-night stand talk.

"I'm sorry. You have a lot on your mind. Maybe it's not the right time to add to it. I don't want to cause any problems."

"Oh no, you're not. He agrees that your company would be a fit for the foundation. That's still a go." Before I can ask, she adds, "Everything else is none of his business."

So, she still wants to go forward with supplying business connections and...What exactly?

"I didn't lie when I said I wanted to see you again, have dinner another time. This...took me by surprise."

I laugh at that. "Yeah, me too."

Kendall studies me curiously. "Any regrets?"

"No." I shake my head for emphasis. "You?"

"My only regret is that we have to wrap this up and talk later. The omelet was delicious."

"Any time."

"I'll call you when I've spoken to someone from the foundation, and when you meet them, we can have dinner afterwards."

"That sounds great."

I see her out, leaning against the door after I've closed it, weak in the knees and not for a good reason. Okay. Deep breath. I'll have to adjust the plan from here.

I might be delusional, but I tell myself that as long as I keep the big picture in mind, this could be to my advantage. For some reason, Kendall doesn't consider me one of her inconsequential one-night stands. She takes an interest in my fake business, so I need to keep her interested.

I can handle the foundation—I have prepped for similar scenarios. An interesting aspect: Kendall and Bruno are not as close as he wishes them to be.

It's been our problem with the Mancini family all along: They, and the people who run with them, are loyal, and have been around for many years. Getting into Kendall's inner circle is still the main objective. If I can drive a wedge between her and Alphonso's right hand man, even better.

She might be more open to trusting me, and sooner. So far, she has invited me to the restaurant, and showed up at my doorstep and and—no, I can't think of that when I'm trying to formulate a plan. It doesn't matter, right?

It's about time that I surprise her.

After cleaning the breakfast dishes, I continue to work on my online profile, together with some research. The radio is on in the background. I jump to my feet and turn the volume higher when I hear the name Marina Fiori.

Even though it's not cold in the apartment, a chill runs through my body. Fiori was found dead, a short time after meeting with Kendall. This can't be coincidence. I know that my colleagues are already on the case, but all of a sudden, I'm afraid of what they might find.

Did someone take offense at the company she kept? Is someone trying to frame Kendall?

There's another, much worse explanation, though I would be naïve to be completely surprised by it. Whatever they shared that night might be so hot that Kendall decided Marina posed a risk. She could have given the order, so no investigation would interfere with her current plans and the long-term business. Does she know that such an investigation is underway?

Every one of those questions is making me queasy.

I can't back out.

———ece———

I dress for a Saturday night out and then call an Uber, have the driver park on the corner rather than take me straight to the address. There's still a light on at *Catania* when I walk through the gate, though it seems the restaurant is empty. How is that possible, at this time of day?

I walk up to the front door and ring the bell.

The man I saw the other day behind the counter answers. He looks as grumpy as he did when I first saw him.

"Hi," I say, trying to sound as cheerful as possible. "I'm Jessica."

"I'm sorry, we're closed now."

"No, please, wait. I'm here to see Kendall. She's here, right?" I know, because I saw her car in the parking lot when I walked from the corner. I can tell from his expression that my intrusion is unexpected and unwelcome—but he doesn't quite know what to do with it. I conclude that Kendall's one-night stands usually don't show up at the family restaurant.

"Wait here," he instructs, and disappears inside the building, all but closing the door in my face.

I wait for a couple of minutes, then five. Eventually, Jimmy Bruno arrives, his irritation unmistakable.

"Ms. Byrne. I take it you didn't call first?"

The entitlement is almost comical. Why is it his business? I can give myself the answer. That's how these clans operate, and Kendall seems surprisingly oblivious after spending all her life in these surroundings. Nothing I learned about Al and Angela tells me Bruno wouldn't be their first choice for son-in-law. It's convenient. It's how things are done.

"I'm sorry. Can I speak to Kendall?"

"She's busy. Maybe you could come back another day."

"Yeah, it looks like it. I'm really sorry." I try to see past him, but he blocks the doorway, only stepping aside when we hear rapid footsteps on the tiled floor.

"Jess, that's a surprise," she says.

"Well...Surprise." I'm acting all happy-go-lucky, but I'm aware of the other vehicles in the parking lot. I don't know who they belong to, but something is happening tonight, and I can't help thinking it has to do with Marina Fiori's death. "Is there somewhere we can talk?"

"Kendall." Bruno's voice holds a warning tone.

"Yeah, it's true that we're a little busy, but I think Jimmy can take care of the rest. I pay him enough over-time. Come on in. Have you had dinner?"

"Oh, no, that wasn't what I meant. I can't eat here for free all the time."

"Well, half of my family does, so don't worry about it. If you must, you can always pay me back."

Kendall has the audacity to wink at me. The tension in the room couldn't be higher...But I'm inside, and Jimmy Bruno will have to learn that I'll be around.

Now all I need is to learn what's going on behind those closed doors.

Chapter Seven

Jess is going to be a complication. I can no longer hide from that fact, though it's not for a lack of trying. I must pay my debts, to my family, the people who have stood by me, even Marina.

Perhaps I owe Jess. The previous night was the first time in a long time I didn't feel like I was suffocating under the crushing weight of responsibility. I won't get any rest unless the people that were taken from me can rest in peace.

Carlo Rossi denies knowing where his father is, or that he was ever present at the fundraiser. That is suspicious.

"Can you wait here a second?" I ask Jess, then go back to the room where we were having that conversation, Jimmy, Carlo and I.

"I want you to understand that we're not after you, or your father. We just want to know the truth about what happened that night. What we do know is that Bianco had a few things over your dad."

He stares back at me defiantly. "So what? I don't answer to you. Get real, Princess, no one does anymore."

Jimmy steps forward, but I hold up a hand to stop him.

"If you came here to repeat the same old sexist bullshit, I don't have time for that. Let me tell you something, Carlo. I don't like men like you. You backed Arturo when he practically sold your sister to the Biancos."

"Sold?" He cackles. "She should have been grateful someone wanted to marry her."

"That right there...My parents never regretted what they did for Sofia, and they were right. She's the only decent human being in your family. Then again, Jimmy doesn't care much about any of this. If Arturo ever talked to you about that night, you better tell us—before the Biancos get wind of any of it."

I nod to Jimmy, and Carlo Rossi doesn't look so cocky anymore. He's probably contemplating what's going to happen to him, and how much it will hurt. I'm not about to have a mess in my restaurant on a Saturday night, but he doesn't know that.

"I have some business to take care of. See you, Carlo."

As I leave the room, I think with regret that some of my own family has apparently fallen for the same sexist bullshit. I need to do something about that. My parents would have had none of it.

I join Jess who has taken a seat at a window table, a glass of wine in front of her.

"Don't worry, I'm going to pay for it," she says. "I'm really sorry for bothering you."

"No problem," I say though that's not entirely true. "What's going on?"

She looks uncomfortable. I'm not sure what to make of it.

"Were you serious when you said you wanted to see me again?"

"Of course. And here you are, so that already worked out."

She smiles hesitantly. I wish I could just abandon all responsibility for a while and take her somewhere, away from the Rossis and Biancos of the world. It's not that I can't handle them, but do I want to? The promise leaves me no choice. I guess that's what you call burnout. The fact that Jimmy is on the verge of booking a wedding venue doesn't help at all.

"I know we talked about the foundation, and that would be a huge step for me."

"I'm sorry I haven't been able to get back to them yet, but I will. I promise." Another promise, though this one isn't forever binding. It's easy to keep.

"I'm glad you didn't do it yet," Jess says, sounding somber. "I've been running my numbers all day, and I'm just not sure if I'm ready for it."

"Oh. Okay." There I thought she was either telling me she changed her mind about us, or she had questions about the rooms behind the counter. Jess has cold feet, but not when it comes to us. The thought fills me with surprising relief—and glee. I don't do glee, normally. I've only known her for a few days, and she's already made a difference. It should be enough to make alarm bells go off. "You won't find out until you make that step though."

"I know." She sighs. "My company is tiny compared to your business, and every step I realize I have a lot to learn."

"I understand. I thought it was tough, and I had the opportunity to grow into it, while my parents were still around. I had to take chances, too, but it's your decision of course. What do you want to do?"

She ponders this for a moment.

"I imagine you deal with a lot of different contractors, and perhaps bigger design firms."

"Sometimes, yes, though I don't do it all in person."

"I was wondering..." For a second or so I'm distracted when she licks her lips though I imagine it's more a sign of nervousness than an attempt at seduction. Works both ways.

"If you could give me some sort of unpaid position, where I could shadow you, learn from you. And it's totally okay if you say no. I'd love to date you regardless."

My answer takes a little too long, and she shakes her head.

"Forget I said that. I know you have a company to run, and unlike me, you are already doing it with success. You don't have time for this, I understand."

"No, wait. Give me a second. That's not what I thought you were going to say. It's actually an excellent idea." I know it's going to piss off some people that should be rallying around me. I'm not above reminding my family, what's left of it, that they, too, owe a debt to my parents. "How about Monday morning, you come by around six and I give you a tour?"

I see her eyes widen a bit, amused at her reaction. If she wants to be in my world, that's how it's going to be. Early mornings.

"That would be amazing." She finishes her glass and puts it on the table. "Again, I'm sorry for coming by unannounced, but not for what came out of it. I'll stop bothering you now, until Monday that is."

"You're not bothering me. Have you eaten yet? Because I haven't—"

I'm interrupted by Carlo storming out, heading right for our table. Judging from his looks, words are all Jimmy used, but they must have been efficient.

"You're going to regret this!" he rages. Jimmy and a member of the security team step in.

"Don't be stupid," Jimmy warns, and they escort him out.

I see Jess following the exchange with interest.

"Unfortunately, that's part of the deal if you're a woman and successful in business." I shrug. "Some people don't like it." Truth be told, Arturo has hated my parents since they took in Sofia, but that's another story for another day—or never.

Jimmy returns to the table, hovering. Another thing I don't need today.

"We're going to have dinner," I inform him. "Thank you for that. Let me know if he's any trouble...Other than that, why don't you take the night off?"

His reaction is almost comical though we both know I'm serious. If I'm going to confront Tony, I need to have my own house in order first. After a few seconds of silent stand-off, he nods.

"I'll see you tomorrow. I'll make sure everything's ready."

With the new information from Carlo, I'll head over to Tony's in the afternoon. Then it's going to be family dinner at my cousin Luca's.

"Thank you. Good night."

He won't like that either, but I think it's a great idea. The time of caution is over. I need to know who's on my side.

This time, I have a waiter bring menus, and while Jessica is studying hers, I say, "I know it's a bit early to meet the family, but is there any chance you'd be free tomorrow night?" Perhaps it's not too strange. She came here, after all.

Jess lays down the menu. "You're right, it is early...When do I need to be ready?" We both laugh, and she adds, "I don't know what to say. Things have become so much more exciting since I met you. That sounds bad, doesn't it? I thought I might be able to hide the small-town girl a bit longer."

"Nothing wrong with coming from a small town. And we've already established that I can show you the ropes."

"How can I ever pay you back?"

I gauge the temperature. "There are ways."

Yes, I was right.

⎯⎯ℓℓ⎯⎯

Some might say it's dangerous, bordering on suicidal even, letting someone new in my life at this specific, difficult point. They might be right.

But Jimmy is no idiot, and if he says Jessica's story checks out, it does. I can't wait to see her again, let alone...Still, I kiss her goodnight and send her home that night. Everything else is for after the dreaded family dinner where I have to establish...something. Dominance. At the very least, respect. I'm going to present someone by my side all right, and I'm not about to lie to myself or anybody for the sensibilities of a few older men, Uncle Lorenzo, or Tony Bianco. My own family should know how much I invested in the business, the family. I need to know that their loyalty is to me, not some archaic ideology. The dinner will be an excellent test.

First of all, Tony.

I don't want to announce my visit, because I don't want to give him time to rehearse his story. I want it low-key, just me and Jimmy, and I'm not above sending him outside if that gets me somewhere with the Bianco patriarch.

He runs his clan like the olden days—women are window dressing. I'm not sure I ever heard his wife say a word, and his daughters and daughters-in-law pretty much behave the same way. If anything, he needs to learn that his time is over, but we'll start with baby steps.

Five minutes to two, Jimmy rings my doorbell and I take the elevator down to the ground floor. He wears sunglasses which earns a frown from me. "Long night, or did you want to look the part?" I ask, but he's not receptive to jokes today, just shrugs.

"You're ready to do this?"

"Of course. Are you?"

I don't like that tone at all, especially given what we are about to do.

"That's not a serious question, is it? If they are hiding away Arturo, and he knows who killed my father, there will be consequences."

"Sure."

"You don't sound convinced."

"You seem distracted lately."

"Because of Jessica? Come on, it's not like you pledged a vow of abstinence when Dad brought you into the family. This is ridiculous. Just because I'm sexually active, it doesn't mean my head's not in the game." I made him cringe, and intentionally so. "But you need to get your act together for this. If you can't, I'll have to find someone else."

"Yes, Ma'am."

I'd like to say more, but we have arrived. "Remember, you're the back-up," I warn him. I might be overreacting lately, but his attitude, and that of other members of the family, bother me. It has to end. After I've found my father's killer, I have other challenges waiting for me.

—ell—

From the looks of it, Tony has family over for dinner as well. The people in the den give us stares ranging from suspicious to openly aggressive. Children are playing in a corner of the large room, oblivious to the sudden tension.

Tony Bianco pretends all of this is perfectly normal, and I'm not surprised.

"Kendall Mancini," he says. "My, you're all grown up." One of his sons can't hold back the grin.

"We need to talk." No point in wasting time with them.

"Do we? It's a little inconvenient, as you can see."

"We do. This involves Arturo, and Carlo."

Just like that, no one is smiling anymore, not even Tony.

"You have ten minutes," he says. "Say your piece, and then leave us alone."

"Works for me."

Jimmy follows us to the door of his office.

"He stays here."

I hold up my hand when Jimmy's about to protest. Tony and I go inside the office, and we take seats in the sitting area by the window.

"You have a lot of nerve, Kendall."

"I could say the same thing about you. You've been talking to Arturo lately? About the fundraiser the night my father was murdered?"

He makes a dismissive gesture with his hand. "I know that you're grieving, and I'm sorry about that. But you better not start any rumors that involve my family and Rossi."

"They wouldn't be rumors if they're true."

"Well, they aren't."

"Arturo was on the guest list. And he was struggling to get back into your good graces after Sofia."

"Two dozen other people were on the guest list, and many of them had a reason for wanting your father out of commission. Not me. I never considered him competition."

I'm on my feet in a heartbeat, and he laughs.

"See, this is why he was always so worried. No son, and his only child is an angry dyke. You can rage against that all you want, but no one will take you seriously. Your own family doesn't. No, we're not afraid of your clan, nor were we ever. And we're not hiding Arturo."

"Carlo says so." I won't waste my breath trying to catch up with all the old man's insults. My time will come.

"He's a coward. Or perhaps someone paid him to say that, to sow division...You find that funny?"

I can't help it. Division is a strange word to describe the relationship between our families, when there was never any unity. We were always on opposite ends.

"Actually, no. If it's any comfort to you, I don't trust Carlo more than I trust you. Marina was killed over that list. I'm looking at everyone who's on it—"

"I'm not."

"And everyone who's related to them. Just so you understand, business is thriving, and I intend to keep it that way. Turns out not everyone is a sexist homophobic dinosaur."

"Very precious. I feel sorry for your lapdog out there, but hey, that's his choice. Contrary to what you might believe, I didn't hate your father. Like I said, he didn't rise to that level of importance to me, though I know he was a family man, and I can appreciate that."

"Spare me."

"You want to know what happened that night? You might want to look at this guy. Blake Ford. He hung around for a while, and they were pretty chummy. You must have seen his name on that list too."

"Blake Ford?" That name does ring a bell though I'm certain he wasn't on Marina's list.

"Your ten minutes are up. Enjoy your Sunday, Kendall."

I'm lost in thought as Jimmy and I walk back to the car.

"So, was that worth it?" he asks.

"I don't know yet." I don't want to talk about it. It's easy to assume Tony was messing with me. I want to be sure before I take further measures.

Chapter Eight

I should be, I don't know, glad? It's obvious to me that
Kendall is taking more or less subtle steps to control
the way our relationship is going. If it puts her at ease,
I'm fine with it. I'm going to meet the family and join her
at headquarters the next day, which is a good amount of
progress. Already I caught the meeting with Carlo Rossi,
son of a man who has tried to play both sides before.

Family dinner—Bruno isn't going to like it. Tonight, I
dress in a more formal way. I assume he will be present,
wondering what Kendall is thinking, presenting her date
in a private setting.

Perhaps I caught her in a weak moment. She seems
tired of the hypocrisy defining this kind of family
organizations that thrive on hyper-masculinity.

Perfect, right? There shouldn't be anything else, not
the sliver of guilty conscience for exploiting her grief, or
the hint of an emotion I can't afford to have.

Attraction. It will help me play my role better.

I thought Kendall might send a driver for the occasion,
but to my surprise, she's picking me up. Looking at her,

I'm glad I opted for conservative but formal wear, which seems to be the theme of the night.

"I'm a little nervous," I admit. "This is soon."

She leans in to kiss me, first my lips, then my neck, while her hand wanders down my side. "You want me to relax you a little?"

"I wish. But then I couldn't look anyone in the eye."

She sits back with a smile and starts the engine. "Later, then."

Yes, later, definitely. I'm in over my head, but who cares if I can produce the wanted results? She can barely claim entrapment when she's all over me the moment we're in the same confined space. Not that I mind, and therein might lie a problem. I have to concentrate on my story and being the plus one that Kendall has envisioned.

Tomorrow, headquarters of the Mancini Group. It's all about the big picture, avoiding a war between the crime families and taking down as many of them as possible in the process.

"I'd like that," I say, carefully reaching out to take her hand when we stop at a red light. She doesn't pull back. For a second or so I can almost make myself believe that we are different people, that I'm simply on a date with a gorgeous woman who's a lot wealthier than I could ever imagine to be.

"Good. I hope they'll behave. If they don't, Uncle Lorenzo is at least generous with excellent wine, and I'll make it up to you later."

"That sounds perfect."

When we arrive, a man about Kendall's age opens the door to us. Their greeting is friendly, I observe.

"Jess, this is my cousin Luca. Luca...Jessica who was brave enough to join me tonight."

"So I've heard," he says as he shakes my hand. "Welcome, Jessica."

"Thank you."

We're not out of our coats yet when Jimmy arrives, glass in hand. I find it interesting that he came here before us. Does that happen all the time? Judging from the way Kendall's face falls, it doesn't.

"Hey, Jimmy," she says. "You're early."

"Just doing my job," he returns. "Ms. Byrne."

"Good evening, Mr. Bruno."

"Call me Jimmy. I get the feeling we'll see a lot more of each other."

I get the feeling there's a jibe in his words, but I ignore it.

"Jimmy it is. I'm Jessica."

"All right, now that we've got that cleared up, where is everyone? Where's the wine?" Kendall asks, unmasked impatience in her tone. Only Luca laughs.

"Come with me," he says.

―――*ele*―――

A lot of handshakes and polite smiles follow, though I can tell the Mancinis have questions.

"It's so nice you could join Kendall," Anna, Lorenzo's wife, tells me. Claudia is here with her husband Marc. Luca brought his wife Elena and their two children. There are two more uncles, one a widower, one with his wife, and a few more cousins. I file away their names and their reactions—and how close they stand to Uncle Lorenzo, and Jimmy.

There is a tug of war going on, no doubt about it.

Kendall is taking a risk, which is as heartening as it might be dangerous.

"Thank you so much for having me."

Anna smiles and squeezes my hand. "Sometimes we need to find family in uncommon places." Lorenzo gives her a warning look, and she stubbornly holds his gaze.

I'm not here to watch this kind of dynamics, but it would be interesting just for them.

Anna seats us in the middle of the giant table, across from Luca who has his wife to the left, Claudia and Marc to the right. Anna and Lorenzo take seats at both ends of the table. I feel like I'm in some old-fashioned movie, but that's the thing—everything in this world is old-fashioned. I'm starting to wonder how tired of it Kendall is, and if there's another way out for her that doesn't lead to a long prison sentence.

When I offer to help, both Anna and Kendall turn me down in no uncertain terms, and I realize that I've come close to a serious *faux-pas*. The younger women help bring in the food. I notice that Luca, too, lends a hand.

With so many people around, including children, it's not exactly a quiet event. I don't stand out as much as I feared.

Kendall whispers to me, "You made an impression."

"Come on." The noise level is high enough that no one cares to eavesdrop on our conversation.

"It's true. And thank you so much for being here."

"I'm glad to be here."

Her smile is both enigmatic and promising. I barely suppress a shiver.

After dinner, Lorenzo offers his sons and nephews a drink in the den, coffee and dessert for the rest of us.

"I think I should be in there," Kendall says when Lorenzo is about to close the French doors.

He looks a bit uncomfortable.

"Don't worry, it's not for the beverage. I saw Tony today."

For a couple of seconds or so, all the adults sit in stunned silence, me included.

She went to see Bianco? I wonder what they talked about. If any threats were made, I can't tell from her demeanor. If anything, she seems thoughtful, serene—not like a war is about to break out anytime soon. It could be an act. In any case, this dinner, the afternoon meeting, and the man storming out of the restaurant's office, they are related.

Looking unhappy, Lorenzo waves her into the den and then closes the doors soundly.

I say yes to coffee and the fresh strawberry cake—to mask my surprise, and because I'll need my strength later.

I wish I could hear what they are saying inside, but the French doors provide privacy for a reason. Sipping my coffee, I turn just enough to see Kendall pacing inside.

"So, where did you and Kendall meet?" Claudia asks.

I can't imagine Kendall told them the truth, so I won't either.

"I moved here recently, and started a small design business," I say. "I was looking for business contacts, and she's been very helpful."

"I can imagine." That comment, close to a sneer, comes from Bruno who has appeared behind us. Kendall is with him.

"Anna, thank you so much for your hospitality. Unfortunately Jess and I have to leave. Something came up."

"Oh. I hope everything is okay?"

"Yes, don't worry. Just work."

"You don't want to stay a little bit longer?" One by one, the men emerge from the den. Luca sounds disappointed.

"I can't. Sorry. I'll call you. Jess?"

I am on my feet, feeling faint regret for having to leave half of the delicious cake behind. Kendall barely waits for me to get into my coat, but when we are in the car, she doesn't start it right away. I flinch when she hits the steering wheel.

"Ouch," I say softly. "Everything is not okay."

She doesn't try to convince me otherwise. "Let's get out of here."

***

Later, I make her laugh when she pulls me close, and the first thing I blurt out is "It was so worth leaving that cake."

"God, I hope so."

I'm still deep in blissful denial, or at least my body is. I haven't been this relaxed in years. Kendall is dealing with her frustration in ways that are extremely pleasant for me.

"I admit I don't understand. You're a successful businesswoman. Why—?"

"Why can't they see that? Because they don't feel like it. Because no one has ever held them accountable, I guess."

Is she talking about Tony Bianco or the extended Mancini family where the men retreat for drinks and shop talk after dinner?

"I'm sorry. I didn't mean to kill the mood."

"You didn't. You're the absolute highlight of my day."

"Thank you. Every story is different, and I'm determined to never tell anyone else how to handle their family...but all of this, it seems old-fashioned."

"That's because it is." She holds my gaze for a long time, amused.

"What?"

"I can tell you're getting all the wrong ideas. Luca's and my generation isn't like that, and you met Anna—she's trying. Uncle Lorenzo can be a pain, but he should know better."

"Like I said, I respect that. You're the expert here."

"But for a moment you thought we were some kind of mafia clan. It's a little bit offensive."

"I...didn't..." I feel the heat rush to my face, not because I think she made me, but because we're in bed naked, and I'd be embarrassed if she thought I fell for some offensive stereotype. At least she's still joking. It's a small comfort.

"Believe me, it wouldn't be the first time. Last names, the family restaurant, and how we came to wealth...Jess, come on. You passed with flying colors."

"Not funny."

"Okay. You're right. I'm sorry." She leans over me and kisses me deeply. "Better?"

"I'm not sure. Try again."

"I really like your place," she says. "But how about we go to mine next time? I'll ask Anna if she has some leftover cake."

"You're spoiling me," I say, my voice jumping a notch on the last word when her fingertips steal between my legs.

"That's the plan."

Chapter Nine

B lake Ford. I sit in my office, frowning at the multiple results my search gets. I need to find this guy, if only to figure out if Tony is playing mind games. It's five a.m., and I haven't had coffee yet. My head hurts. Maybe the pain is in other places, the omnipresent grief, the regrets over many things.

I tried to joke about my family's antics, but the truth is they weren't funny. Uncle Lorenzo scolded me like I was a schoolgirl for talking to Bianco. I am not shy about talking back, but did he really get the message? Did he know my parents at all, did he respect my mother's authority after my father's death?

I have more doubts than I can handle at the moment. It's the worst timing to think about whether it's time to replace Jimmy. It would be hard to do, especially now, but he's getting on my last nerve.

I guess I'll have to live with that a little while longer, given that my parents put so much trust in him. I consider calling Anna, but after a look to my watch I decide to send her a message and ask her to call me back instead.

Jimmy arrives at 5:30 a.m. with two tall coffees and a double chocolate muffin. At least he read the room correctly and understood he messed up.

"That's a bit easy for an apology, but since it's Monday morning, and I have a long day ahead, I'll take it."

He smiles ruefully. "I'm sorry if I've been hard on you. I'm worried."

"You don't need to worry about me, or Jess for that matter, and you're right, she'll be around. In fact, she'll be here at 6 a.m. so I can show her the ropes."

I can tell he's barely holding back a retort. I'll give him credit for managing to do so.

"You really want to do business with her?"

"She could use a little guidance. I can provide that."

"You must know."

"I do. Listen, I was wondering if you remember Blake Ford."

He sits up straighter immediately. "What about him? You found him?"

That, I did not expect.

"Tell me about this guy."

"I thought you knew the story. He was a contractor Alphonso worked with for a while."

"Was?"

Why do I have such trouble remembering him?

"It was during the time when you were mostly working with the Adria Group. Al liked him a lot, and he came to dinner at *Catania*. They became friends. You must have met him once or twice."

That makes more sense—I was still busy proving myself at the time, but I think I have an image, a friendly older guy with a faint accent. He was around. I remember him and my dad laughing together. He had a son if I remember correctly.

"Yes, I did. His name wasn't on the list Marina gave me. Why would Tony bring him up?"

"He did?" Jimmy drinks his coffee, leaving the question hang in the air for a moment. "You think Tony might have planted him? If that's the case, he's pretty bold."

"Bold is a mild word to describe him, but I'll give him some credit after what I heard from Uncle Lorenzo. He can't be serious."

Jimmy shrugs, signaling he's not going to wade into that territory with me on a Monday morning. "Bianco isn't your family though. The thing about Ford, he helped Al make some connections, I think, but mostly they became friends. Then all of a sudden, he vanished without a trace. He didn't even come to the funeral as far as I remember."

"What you're saying is Dad likely shouldn't have trusted him."

"I'm not sure, but the timing was odd."

"You didn't go to that fundraiser, why?"

I can see the alarm in his face. "Kendall."

"Relax. You just never told me why."

He avoids my gaze when he says, "It was stupid. I could have gone, and maybe I would have been able to...I don't know. I was on a date. Al wasn't too happy about it, and not because I was missing the fundraiser."

For some things to ignore, a chocolate muffin is not enough.

"Not that again."

"I'm not kidding. He felt like I was betraying you."

"That's your imagination. He knew we were never going to be anything but business partners." I sigh before I take a sip of the coffee that's now lukewarm. "But if it makes you feel any better, you have my blessing to go on any date you want. You're right, the timing was odd. I need to talk to that Ford guy. It can't be a coincidence he disappeared after the shooting."

"I'll look into it."

The doorbell makes me jump, as if I'd been doing something forbidden.

"That's Jess," I say. "Let me know if you find anything."

He nods and gets up to leave as I buzz her in.

Jess brings me coffee and a Danish, which is both amusing and charming, a sign of things to come. I might have to change my exercise routine if those two keep it up.

"I'll take the coffee. This is my lunch, I guess. I just had breakfast."

"Oh, I'm sorry, I didn't mean—"

"It's fine, but you don't need to do this. You're not my assistant."

"Got it," she says with a smile. "So, what are we doing?"

"Lots of boring paperwork, I'm afraid. A meeting at noon, conference call at 2:30. I'll have to do a few more calls, but you can take a break whenever you want."

"Sounds great."

"I've arranged to meet with a designer on site. That might be the most interesting thing for you."

"That is awesome. Let me know what I can do."

It's daring to keep her close, but also the most pragmatic thing to do. Jimmy doesn't think so, but it's the perfect solution. What I'm showing her will be helpful. It barely scratches the surface of things behind the curtain, and that's the way I want it.

It's much too early to tell if we could have something, in the future. I can't afford any bad surprises while we figure it out. Jess is someone good in my life. I need that now.

When Sue, my real assistant, comes in, I take her aside after introducing the two.

"Maybe you could find something for her to do, updating one of the databases, organizing? Something that reflects the organization and the work we do here."

Sue gives me a cordial smile. Of course, she can. "No problem."

"Good. She'll join me in the meeting at noon, but I think I'll catch up with you sooner."

When I have a moment alone, I try to call Jimmy, but the call goes to voicemail. I wish I could talk to Mom, ask her about Ford. I want to ask her about so many things, but time ran out.

At least Luca's going to be in the meeting. I need all the allies I can get.

Chapter Ten

I n her office, Kendall is tackling the phone calls she talked about while Sue gets me settled in an empty cubicle. Just like that.

"You'll get to the more exciting part of the day later. For now, could you just add these..." With a few clicks, she brings up a spreadsheet. I notice that there's almost nothing on the computer.

Any computer will do.

So far, so easy.

"Thank you so much," I beam at Sue as if I'm really the woman so eager to throw in the towel that she's taking a boring entry-level job at her lover's company. Well, internship. Unpaid.

"No problem. Ms. Mancini is always willing to help out," she says before settling behind her own desk.

I wonder if Ms. Mancini prepared Sue for my arrival. It doesn't matter now. I won't disappoint her—not today. The moment will come soon enough.

"I'll be back in a few minutes," Sue says behind me, and I realize that almost an hour has gone by. Maybe I'm in for a new career?

I suppress a nervous giggle, a good idea when Kendall appears in front of me all of a sudden.

"Hey. How's it going?" I ask.

"So far so good," she says vaguely. "You?"

"I'm busy."

"Yeah, sorry about that. We have lots of moving pieces at the moment, but I swear it will be more fun when we get to the site later."

"Don't worry about it," I say, my heart beating fast. "This is interesting."

"All right. I have to go talk to someone, and then I'll show you something more interesting."

Did she just wink at me?

I have no time to contemplate her insinuations, or my reaction to them. When she's out the door, I turn back to my screen. I lied. There's nothing interesting here, but of course they wouldn't present anything to me on a silver platter.

Kendall Mancini and I have arrived at the stage in our relationship where I have to do something unforgivable: My job.

I've been part of operations like this before. They were on a slightly smaller scale, but the principles remain the same. Get as close as you can, and then get as much as you can within the law.

I can feel myself starting to sweat as I insert the small device into the USB slot. It all seemed so easy when the tech guy explained it to me. Wait until it's done, send the text.

The waiting is the problem. Either Kendall or Sue will be back within the next few minutes...What the hell is taking so long? This is supposed to be modern, state-of-the-art surveillance equipment.

I can see the small clock counting down the longest thirteen seconds of my life, then I'm in. Not long, and I can see that there are many more folders. I'm not here to look at them now.

I take the device out and put it back into my purse the moment Jimmy Bruno walks into the office.

"Where is everyone?" he asks, sounding irritated.

"They didn't tell me where they were going, but I think either Kendall or Sue will be back in a few minutes. Can I help you?"

He scoffs at that and turns to go inside Kendall's office while I try to calm my breathing. That was close.

Interesting things are happening, no doubt about it. I'll send the message later when I am less exposed: *Thanks, Mom. See you at dinner.*

What I want to know is why he's in there by himself, frowning at the computer screen as he's typing away.

Any computer will do.

Eventually he gets up and leaves without any explanation.

I pick up one of the folders Sue gave me earlier and head over to Kendall's office, where I try my key card. No, it doesn't work. It's not that easy.

I wonder what Jimmy was doing though. Earlier when I was preparing for my assignment, we looked into his finances too, finding nothing other than the right hand man is being paid well.

One of the agents argued that trying to turn him might make more sense. I don't think so, and not just because I wanted to be the one to succeed with Kendall. He's ruthless. He doesn't give a damn if there isn't a reward for him in it, and for sure he wouldn't give up Kendall as long as he still has those unrealistic hopes about his happily ever after with her.

The blood shoots to my face.

Projection, much?

Sue returns to her desk, still no sign of Kendall.

"Could I ask you a favor?"

She shrugs. "Ms. Mancini says you can take a break anytime. The break room is down the hall, there's always fresh coffee and snacks."

"Thank you, but...I'm afraid I left my phone in Kendall's office earlier, and I'm expecting a call. Stupid, I know, but I don't know when she'll be back."

"That's all right, we can check."

Of course, she's coming with me. There's no phone, but I catch a quick glimpse at some papers on the desk. It shouldn't surprise me that Jimmy is involved in financial transactions and comes and goes like he owns the place...but this might be worth a closer look.

"Are you sure this is where you left it?"

The phone on her desk rings, and she hesitates.

"I just need another second. I swear I won't disturb anything..."

"You can go now, Sue," Kendall has appeared behind us, her expression revealing nothing. Sue hurries to answer the phone.

"You need anything?" Kendall asks.

"Actually...no. I'm sorry. I thought I left my phone in here, but I can't see it."

"Maybe we should empty your purse. Things get lost in there sometimes."

I laugh a little. "Yes, but I looked already. Come to think of it, I probably left it at home. Today is an exciting day. Thank you for this."

"Well, the better part of it is coming up. Would you like to have lunch?"

It's a bit early, but I could use a change of scenery, try to calm down. I did what I was supposed to do. Getting more dirt on Jimmy is for extra credit, but I've only been here a day.

___ele___

Out of the office, Kendall too is more relaxed, reminiscent of the woman I met at the bar. Attentive. Flirty.

"I didn't realize Jimmy had this big of a job," I say.

According to her expression, my statement has the quality of a cold shower.

"Why are you saying that?"

"He came over earlier and stayed quite a while in your office."

She shrugs. "Well, yeah, this is somewhat normal. Basically, it's his job to make my life easier. Lately that's a bit relative."

"The easier life, or him providing it?"

"Both," Kendall admits with a sigh. "But let's forget about him and business for a while, okay?"

I can't say no to her. One day that could be disastrous for me, or her, but I push the thought aside.

I have a job to do. Moving parts, there's no denying. With what I did today, my colleagues will have unprecedented access to the world of Mancini.

It will change everything.

Chapter Eleven

W e're visiting the site of one of our developments. This one is an exception, a series of model homes. It's almost finished, and we're visiting one of the homes with the designer.

"This is beautiful." Jess practically radiates happiness. "It leaves so much room for individual taste."

"We only want happy customers," I say.

"True," the designer agrees. "It's a great time to be in the business. There will always be trends, but we have so many options to choose from. You'll never run out of ideas."

"I'm hoping to do big projects like this someday."

"Maybe it doesn't have to be someday, when you're already on the radar of one of the best."

Okay, she doesn't need to do the flattery. We've given her contracts for years and will continue to do so. It's a good flow of energy and money, and this is what we always strive for. Maybe, someday, I can go below the surface with Jess and teach her some of the tricks, especially if she sticks around...but that's a daydream at the moment.

I can't be distracted.

I have to admit that perhaps Jimmy had a point.

I'm not going to tell him. He's overestimating himself as it is.

———*ℓℓ*———

Despite the new addition to the team, the day passes by without any incident. I could live like this, the almost normal life...but there's a lot to take care of before that can happen.

It's just as well that I keep Jess close, at work and at home.

I watch her talk to Sue who has a good eye for new talent. I'm not sure that's what Jess will be. It's a bit odd, this non-sequitur from wanting to make it in her field to shadowing me at work.

I truly believe that she's searching for something—aren't we all? I want to give her the opportunity to bide her time until she has figured it out, and until I have figured out what place she might take some time in the future.

And why not?

Many of the men in my family have had affairs. I am not cheating on anyone. Me enjoying the presence of a beautiful woman while taking care of business is a whole lot less entitled than their actions, and I'll still get the job done.

Chapter Twelve

At the end of the week, I walk around in my apartment in PJs, glass of wine and my burner phone in hand. I can't speak to anyone, not yet, though the coded message I received from "Mom" reveals that the results of one week of surveillance are promising.

I've always known, but the data the team is analyzing now is confirmation that there's a lot more going on than meets the eye. Of course, Kendall doesn't share that information freely, nor does Sue, or the designer—or anyone in that firm.

Some of the records of the Mancini group and Adria tell a story if you know where to look.

High quality food in their restaurants, high quality builds and designs...My team at the field office will do the most work, tackling encrypted files and codes. I expect that the numbers won't add up, though that's not enough yet.

It's no surprise to anyone that Kendall and other members of her family could be indicted for tax evasion.

Jessica Byrne's job is more complex than that. If the powers that be didn't think a war could break out at any moment, leading to a high number of casualties, we could have never gotten the warrant. I'll get it done.

It didn't have to include sex, but here we are.

Sunday morning, I leave the apartment building through the backdoor, wearing clothes more appropriate for a day on the couch than for up-and-coming designer Jess Byrne. I slip away unseen and take a subway across town.

I walk into a coffee shop where I order a cappuccino. Hampton has asked to meet which is exciting, and potentially dangerous. When my order is ready, I find a seat and call him. I tell him the address and nothing else before I end the call.

Hampton arrives exactly sixteen minutes later. He, too, is wearing casual clothes. He orders a black coffee at the counter, and then takes a seat on one of the barstools. The place is full enough that him choosing a seat close to mine doesn't look deliberate. He takes a laptop out of his bag and powers it up.

"We found a lot already. You have to get ready to get out soon."

That is surprising...and too soon. This has been months in the making.

I look at my phone as I say, "I could give you more, but I need time. Any leads on the Fiori murder?"

"We brought in Carlo Rossi. He's denying, but we have DNA."

Arturo Rossi's son. Things are moving on that end, good. I slip from the stool, picking up my drink.

"I have a feeling about Bruno," I say. "Let me find out more. I'll call you when I can."

"Robyn, wait a second. Are you sure you're okay?" He's talking to the screen, not my face, but even so I can't ignore the concern.

"Perfect. See you later."

My face is still burning when I stand on the platform waiting for my train. His instincts are usually right on the money, and I know he doesn't exaggerate, or patronize.

If there's something off about me, it might have to do with the fact that I crossed lines days within my assignment. I'm still telling myself it's all for the sake of the job, and that it will help me get to know Kendall better.

I've begun to wonder what it would take for her to turn.

I can't wait to see her again.

Stupid.

Dangerous.

—ece—

I continue to shadow her at work for another week, taking notes for my own business, so to speak. Kendall stays until after the last employee has gone home, and she is always first in the morning, nothing if not a control freak.

Friday evening, she makes an exception, because we finally go on the date that is going to end at her apartment.

I wait outside her office for her to finish a call, fitting myself against the wall when I hear Bruno's voice. It's coming from the hallway, just around the corner.

"Arturo, no." There's a pause, and I realize he's on the phone. "She doesn't know, and we don't need to bother her with it, right?"

I'm certain he's talking about Kendall. This could be my breakthrough, a real one.

"Not a good idea. Stay where you are until all of it blows over."

He turns the corner, a flash of anger on his face when he sees me, but Kendall emerges from her office at the same moment.

"Ready?" she asks.

"Oh yes. I'm starving."

"Good. I know just the place. Jimmy."

"Making it an early night?" he asks. "That's unusual."

"Nothing here that won't be there tomorrow. I'll be in around noon, for a couple of hours."

"Enjoy your evening," he says stiffly, casting me a quick suspicious glance.

I smile, signaling that I'm harmless and oblivious, just the boss's girlfr...date. There's no reason to use any other term, now or ever.

We have a driver tonight, but I'm still surprised when Kendall opens a bottle of champagne in the backseat.

"What are we celebrating?" I ask.

She hands me a glass with a shrug. "Freedom. Clarity. Honesty. All the things that seem so elusive. Life is too short."

I'm not sure I'm following, but I'm worried about what Hampton told me. I need more time. The more proof I can come up with, the more leverage we have. Kendall might run a tight ship, but she's more in denial about her family than I thought. This could mean...Something. If she could deliver some heavyweights, and I'm sure she could, there are some scenarios we'd be able to avoid.

"I'll drink to that. I'm having a great time watching you at work," I say. "I really admire you."

"I'm not saying I don't like flattery, but there was luck in it. I didn't exactly start at zero. But let's not talk about work for a while."

I stopped at home to change before I came back to headquarters. Kendall, of course, has a small apartment adjacent to her office for these occasions.

Tonight, we dine at one of the restaurants belonging to the Adria Group. Like their parent company, the Mancini group, they make a ton of money, and closed doors deals with all sorts of public figures and celebrities. Yes, if we play our cards right, and Kendall does too, she could come out of it better than I originally imagined.

It's silly of me that I like the idea, as if I'd wait for her, or she'd want me to. Once she learns the truth, she'll never speak another word to me—outside of an interrogation room.

"Don't make that face," she says. "I promise you those elevators never get stuck. Quality work, remember?"

We are in the lobby of an 80-story-building, one of three of the highest in the city, about to step into the elevator to go up to the restaurant at the top, the Adria flagship.

"I'll try to," I say, going with the convenient misunderstanding. Brazen, to take me to the family restaurant and tell me a story about the humble beginnings of the family.

Nothing about Kendall Mancini is humble, in business or in bed. She brushes my hair aside and kisses my neck. "Or maybe it could be fun to spend a little time in here."

I see her expression in the mirror wall and realize she's serious. A pleasant shiver skitters down my spine, but it's not enough to make me consider the option.

"There must be cameras in here."

"Yes, there are," she says with audible regret. "Besides, you said you were hungry."

"I am," I confirm, and then her mouth is on mine, and we kiss until the doors open. For a few seconds there, I wasn't thinking about food.

"Good evening, Ms. Mancini," the hostess greets us the moment we step inside the restaurant. I have a comfortable income, and I've eaten in some good restaurants, comforting places like *Catania*, and gourmet restaurants.

The Adria is out of my league, still, and my jaw drops ever so slightly as the woman guides us to our table right next to the windows. The restaurant covers the whole floor, so views are 360 degrees. Below us, the city in lights.

"You like it?" Kendall asks as if she was responsible for the placement of every single lightbulb in this magical panorama. Like I said—not the humble type.

"It's so beautiful. Unreal," I admit.

"I don't have time to come here often, and, of course, if I need comfort food, I'll go to *Catania*. But this is a great place. You still trust me?"

"I never stopped." I'm not enjoying lying to her face so much, but what can I do? I'll make it up to her in other ways. The fact that I even feel like owing her should alarm me. The thought doesn't make it past the bliss that's about to come my way.

"Good. I have something special planned for us," she says, smiling to the waitress who arrives to present the wine. "Thank you."

Even though there are other people, the sounds seem muted, the acoustics of the room designed for privacy. When I mention this to Kendall, she says, "It's interesting, right? My great-grandparents were really proud of *Catania*, and I understand why. It was a huge step for them. My grandparents realized that combining the restaurant business and real estate made a lot of sense."

"Each generation was able to dream bigger." Or became smarter at hiding away money from the government, funneling it through an ever-expanding network of dark channels. In many ways, our views of the world are similar, but the political contributions the Mancinis make are still dark money. They're not exactly Robin Hood. And none of this is news to me.

"True. What do you dream about, Jess?"

"I'm not sure anymore. I'm living in a dream already."

That part is not a lie, though I already know there will be a rude awakening for both of us, sometime soon.

I think back to the call I overheard and decide it's too soon to mention it. It could be an interesting bargaining chip when I get Jimmy Bruno alone.

After a fabulous menu the driver brings us to Kendall's condo. The view from here isn't the same as from the Adria, but it's close enough to impress. The lovingly designed rooms scream luxury.

"I know you're rich, don't get me wrong, but how rich exactly?"

She laughs. "I'm comfortable, but you guessed that already."

I stand by the window, watching our reflection. "I'm sorry, that was kind of a stupid question. I guess I've just never been around this much luxury."

"And now you are. Don't question it. Just...enjoy." Her hand brushes over my shoulder, down my arm. My breath catches in my throat. Her touch is unhurried, gentle, deliberate. I stand still, as she pulls up the skirt of my dress.

"Perhaps...We should get away from the window?"

"No one can see us," she assures me. "But I see your point. Let's go somewhere more comfortable. I have one more surprise for you."

I almost expect something kinky, but when she leads me to the spacious bedroom, I see nothing of the kind. The drapes are closed in here, the lights dimmed. I wonder if she prepared the room earlier, knowing that we'd come here after dinner. Kendall doesn't leave much to chance.

"Really? What is that?"

"There are a few things I need to take care of next week," she says. "Depending on how that goes, I could show you another family property. I'm thinking of a weekend getaway far from the city."

That is...interesting. It might be a test. I don't think she'd announce it if she were planning to kill me. The Mancini family uses more refined methods, I guess.

"You don't have to give me gifts like that. I can never pay you back."

"You are doing much more than you think. Please."

I'm out of my dress, her heated gaze on me.

I'll have to contact Hampton, and then see what I can find out from Bruno.

"Yes," I whisper. "I'd love to come with you."

Chapter Thirteen

J ess is asleep next to me when Jimmy sends me the copy of a photograph, a party from a few years ago. I zoom in on it on my phone, ignoring the pang of pain. My parents, Uncle Lorenzo, Claudia, and the infamous Blake Ford. He has his face partly turned away from the camera, but he's smiling like everyone in that picture. He was obviously someone my family considered safe. What happened? Did he die? Or was there something more sinister going on, something he did that led to my father's death? If so, why didn't anyone ever raise the question?

I give myself the answer: That night changed all of us. Mom called me shortly after midnight, crying so hard I could barely understand her. Once the smoke lifted and we needed to think of the future of the business, no one even mentioned Ford.

He's a ghost.

But I'm not afraid of any enemy. If this man is still alive, he'll have to answer to me, one way or another.

*　*　*

Strange to think that I might be close to solving the mystery at a time when my life has taken this unexpected turn. Jess might think she's solely here to learn from me, but I'm watching her too, vetting her. Jimmy became a "friend of the family" at a young age. Everyone now considers him family.

Jess handled the dinner graciously, and the closer I get to this point of clarity, the more I need someone close to me that I can trust, not just with the business matters. But of course, those are important.

The upcoming weekend getaway might be a way to slowly introduce her to more of my complicated reality. I already know she won't bolt. It's too far from the city.

I can't wait.

Whatever revelations I'll make—or not—it will be uninterrupted time with her. The thought has become addictive to me. I might be falling for her.

Chapter Fourteen

I feel giddy. I shouldn't. When I go on that retreat with Kendall, I have to be more careful than ever. If the head of a crime family invites you to a remote location, that's always a reason to be cautious.

She seems to be overwhelmed, warding off conflict from all sides, her uncle, the Biancos, the Rossis. Arturo who talks to Jimmy, but not her, was present the night Al Mancini died. His son was arrested for the murder of Marina Fiori.

I would want to get away if I was her.

At 5.55 a.m., we're still in bed, entwined. I have already changed some of her habits.

Me? I shouldn't feel this warm and safe in her embrace...or giddy. But it's for the greater good, right?

"I have to get up," she murmurs against my neck, making no attempt to move.

"Would it bother you if we arrived at the office at the same time?"

"What? No. It's no one's business, though I'm sure everyone knows already." Kendall sits up, a rare vulnerability in her expression. "I never brought a woman to Uncle Lorenzo's," she said.

"You brought a man?"

"A couple of times, many years ago. It wasn't anything serious, and besides, Mom and Dad had their eyes on Jimmy until the moment I came out to them."

I have the feeling we might not make it to the office so soon. I'll have to be careful. If I keep Jimmy's secret too long, it might backfire on me.

"How did that go?"

"Okay, I guess," she says. "No one cried or threatened to disown me." With a laugh she adds, "It might have helped that they didn't have anyone else to give the business to. Some of my uncles might have disagreed, but my parents had the authority."

"I'm sure it wasn't just about the business. They loved you."

"If you grow up like I did, the business is synonymous with family."

"Business school wasn't your choice?"

"Oh, it was. I loved it. I love what I do."

That was the impression I got. Kendall isn't sorry about her luxury life. As far as the real estate business and the restaurants go, she puts a lot of hard work into it. I've seen it up close. But if that was all, I wouldn't be here.

"I can tell, watching you. It's been inspiring."

"Really? You've inspired me too," she says, drawing the sheet aside.

"I thought you said you had to get up..."

"I'm the boss, remember? They'll make do without me another hour or so."

It's an offer too good to refuse.

Later that day, I take a break with a coffee and a pastry in the kitchen adjacent to the office. Kendall is in a meeting I didn't need to attend—her words. Obviously, she trusts me enough to leave me alone in these rooms. I already searched them, installed the software. So far, nothing alarming has happened here.

I believe the family restaurant, and dinners, are the spaces to watch, those times when attendees are separated by gender. Ridiculous, yes, but it also serves a purpose.

At first, I thought it was just Jimmy looking into his options. But if she doesn't act soon, they might try to force her out.

There could be other ways, and the weekend will be the perfect timing to discuss some of them. Kendall is so much more complex than I could have gathered from my research, before meeting her in person. I'm convinced there is a future for her without these men if she wants it.

I've decided not to contact Hampton regarding the getaway. I can take care of myself.

"All by yourself again?"

I jump, almost knocking over my coffee when Jimmy stands in front of me.

"Hey. I thought you were in the meeting with Kendall. I didn't steal anything," I add, trying to make a joke. He's not laughing. "She told me I could take a break, get coffee and a snack in here."

"Yeah. Sure."

I don't think I need to say anything to that. To my surprise, he gets a coffee for himself and then pulls himself a chair.

"You and Kendall are going to the cabin this Friday."

"That's the plan."

He smiles, and I'm immediately alarmed. This guy never smiles at me. I'm aware of the reason.

"Since you'll be around, perhaps you and I should get to know each other better." Implying that he, too, will be around. I get the message.

"You must already know everything there is to know about me after the background check you ran on me."

"Touché. But there's a limit as to what you can learn about a person from their life on paper, wouldn't you say?"

Is he fishing, or am I in trouble?

"True. So, what would you like to know?" I'm not surprised he doesn't answer a direct question.

"I've been around Kendall for a long time. I care about her."

"And she's aware of that. I do too. Is this the talk where you tell me not to break her heart? I don't plan to, but Jimmy, she's a grown woman. I don't think she'd appreciate this."

"She knows I'm looking out for her. Anyway, you probably noticed she has a lot going on now. All I want is for you to be respectful of her obligations."

"I am, don't worry."

"She's been coming in later, leaving earlier lately."

"Oh, come on. You really think I could convince her to do that if she didn't want to?"

That amuses him.

"You're right about that. Enjoy your cake, Jessica."

"Hang on."

Already by the door, he turns around.

"I understand you're just trying to protect her, but you don't have to worry about me. I like her...a lot. That's why I get it."

"Get what?"

"That in order to protect her, you sometimes have to keep secrets from her. Like Arturo Rossi. I heard that the police arrested his son, and I imagine Kendall cannot be close to all of this."

I have his attention now.

He comes back to stand in front of me.

"Whatever you heard, or you think you heard, that's none of your business."

"Like I said...I assume you have your reasons."

"Don't assume. Keep your mouth shut and don't meddle in things you don't understand. As long as you keep Kendall happy, you're useful around here. That can change. Don't forget it."

"Understood."

"Is it?"

He doesn't wait for an answer, just shakes his head and leaves. I made my move. The next few days will be interesting.

I don't get to have time alone with Kendall until after hours. It's late, but she's still sitting at her desk going over papers. After a few minutes, she looks up at me with regret.

"I don't think I'll have time for dinner today. You can go home if you want."

"I guess I'll do that...but there's something I wanted to run by you if you don't mind."

"Sure, I have a few minutes."

She's so business-like, in control, within these four walls. The more private, laid-back Kendall I've come to know seems far away. Though she likes control in every aspect of her life.

"Arturo and Carlo Rossi, are the two related? You know them?"

"Why do you want to know?"

"I heard about one of them being arrested."

"That's Carlo, Arturo's son. I'm not surprised."

"Why do you say that?"

"They're bad news. As to your question, yes, I'm aware of them, but I'd never do business with any of them. Arturo married off his daughter to an abuser, and he and Carlo never forgave her for daring to want out of that relationship." Her unveiled anger confirms some of what

I already know—and some of what I want to think, like her heart is in the right place? That would be pathetic.

Her reaction is encouraging. I have to stay on track.

"Wow. Okay. Then there would be no reason for anyone here to speak to either one of them."

Kendall frowns. "What's that supposed to mean?"

I hesitate. "I'm not sure I'm supposed to tell you, but after what happened today, I'm not comfortable keeping it from you. Especially with what you're telling me now."

"Stop being vague. What happened today?"

"Yesterday I accidentally overheard Jimmy talking to Arturo Rossi."

"What? No. Fuck." Kendall doesn't use expletives often, but this situation seems to call for one. I'm curious.

"I'm sorry I didn't tell you earlier. But today, when I was in the kitchen, Jimmy told me to keep my mouth shut, that it was none of my business..."

"I can't believe this. Jess. It's a good thing you told me. We'll have a lot to talk about on the weekend, but...damn it. He's been going out of his way to piss me off, and now this?"

"I'm sorry," I offer once more.

"Yes, me too. You have no idea. I know Jimmy is near paranoid, but he should know better when it comes to the Rossis. My parents took in Sofia, Rossi's daughter, when she had nowhere to go. They've been trying to sabotage us ever since."

With the help of the more powerful Biancos. I don't think it's a coincidence that she leaves out that name. The abuser was Tony Bianco's son, still coddled by his family.

I know Kendall is tired. I am too. The enthusiasm I had in the beginning, about doing right, about bringing them all down, is vanishing. Not everyone is equally guilty in this.

Focus.

"But you trust Jimmy. I suppose he has a plan here."

"That doesn't mean he can talk to you like that. I'll have to have a conversation..."

"Oh, no, please don't tell him I gave you details. He'll be angry I let you know about the phone call anyway."

"He can be angry all he wants. It's about time someone put him in his place. I want to talk to Luca as well. I think it's time to shift responsibilities."

Jimmy Bruno will be mad as hell. A good part of the job is done. One more thing though.

"Arturo, if he hates your family so much, do you think he was involved in your father's death?"

It might be a step too far. However, Kendall gives me a smile I'm not sure how to interpret.

"You don't understand everything, Jess. The Rossis are small fish, though we have to watch them. I hope that's what Jimmy is doing." Her expression turns somber. "No one knows who killed my dad. The police were never much help in this."

"That must have been terrible."

I have done undercover work before. I understand that the target is a person that comes with their own history, grief, regrets, but I know that I have to push that concept aside. They've committed crimes. They should be held accountable even if they themselves are hurting. I still believe that, but I also know Kendall's story, and losing her father, is central to my assignment.

She takes a long time to answer, as if it's extremely important to find the right words.

"It was. It still is. My mother never got over it. I hated to lose her too, but she almost seemed relieved."

Loving someone so much that you can't imagine living a day without them? I can't afford to get lost in someone else's love story. Hampton and my other colleagues are working on the information they're getting from the software now. With each file and bank statement, we're getting closer to making arrests.

"You have a lot on your shoulders. What do you need?"

"You are helping more than you can imagine," she says. I take a step forward, and she wraps her arms around me, holding on tightly. "I'm changing my mind. If you want to stay, I'll have someone prepare dinner for us? I'll still have to work, but we can have it delivered here. Anything from *Catania* or Adria you want."

"I'll be here for you. And please, let me pay for something for a change."

"If that's what it takes to make you happy."

She brushes a hand over my hair. "You can't imagine how much I look forward to going to the cabin, but there's a lot left to do. I might have figured out who had a hand in my father's death."

I step back. "What do you mean? Isn't that dangerous? You should leave that to the police."

"They haven't done much for me so far, but this is part of what I need to explain to you on the weekend. His name is Blake Ford. He pretended to be my father's friend, but it turned out he was anything but that. If he pulled that trigger—he took everything from my family. Someone needs to hold him accountable."

"Kendall. Be careful."

It's a good thing that even as Jess, I have legitimate reason to be upset, because on the inside, I'm shaking. This can't be right. I know the name, and I know who used it. And he shouldn't have been anywhere near the fundraiser where Mancini was shot, allegedly by law enforcement.

Damn it.

"I will be. Don't worry about me. Let's get something to eat now. Is pizza okay with you?"

Chapter Fifteen

I meant to sleep in my own bed tonight, but that's not going to happen. It might be better that way. I'm not going to do anything ill-advised. Things have been going according to plan—I have evidence. Kendall admitted to me that she's still hell-bent on revenge against whoever killed her father, and Jimmy looks to be on his way out.

She's begun to tell me details.

I don't know what to believe. Is that the reason why my own father resigned abruptly, shortly after the night Mancini died? As far as I know, he didn't suffer any consequences, but there's been a veil of silence over that operation. Even with the access I had, I didn't always feel like I had the whole story.

I might be one step closer to it, and I have no idea what to do. I'm sure Dad could answer a lot of questions, but I can't contact him in the middle of this assignment—too dangerous for him and me.

Hampton? Like me, he joined our field office after the incident, so he's unlikely to know more than I do. I can't believe that the people I've worked with, that I've looked up to, would sweep something like that under the carpet—and why?

Whatever went down that night, I know my father isn't reckless. If he shot Mancini, it was for a reason.

Of course, Kendall won't see it that way, and potentially all my plans to get her to turn on Bruno and the rest of the family will have become unrealistic.

There's only one way—I need to learn what happened. And then I have to make sure she never finds out that Blake Ford and I are connected.

The thought of what she is planning on her side is terrifying. No, I can't just let it be. I need to involve other people, to protect my parents. All of a sudden, it's easy to understand why Kendall is so driven, so determined to make things right the way she thinks is necessary. It's a surprise that despite all those disturbing thoughts, I slip into a restful sleep next to her.

I wake up to the early morning light to find her watching me.

"This is...nice. Also, a bit creepy."

Kendall laughs. "I'm sorry, I couldn't help myself." She leans in to kiss me. I should be alarmed, put off, given what I've learned, but my body remains a traitor.

"That seems to happen a lot with you," I tease, but reluctantly remove myself from her embrace.

"I thought we could have breakfast here?" she asks, her tone strangely worried.

"I'm sorry, I have to go to my apartment. Take a shower, change, before I come to the office."

Are we pathetic? I'm almost disappointed that she's not trying harder. But I have somewhere to be, and I only have a small window of time.

"I guess I have to let you go then."

"Weekend's almost here. Then you'll have me all to yourself."

A half hour later, I'm at my apartment. I search it regularly to avoid bad surprises, but this is too delicate. I leave once again to take the train across town. I don't have the hope that Hampton can meet me before I have to show up at Mancini headquarters, but he can get the ball rolling. He has to.

To my relief, he answers after only two rings.

"Is everything okay?" are his first words.

"Yes. Maybe not. You need to talk to the boss."

"Robyn, you gave us access to a goldmine of information. We could take in Mancini and Bruno right away."

"It's not enough. I'll get you more." Somehow it doesn't seem fair that Kendall should take the fall by herself when the homophobic sexist part of her family has done their criminal part. She told me we had to talk on the weekend—no kidding. I need to take a risk, before she digs up more on Blake Ford. "But I need a favor from you. They are starting to look into everyone who attended the fundraiser. Did you know that my father was there? You need to make sure my family is protected."

"I'll talk to the boss," he promises. "We'll sort it out, don't worry."

It doesn't go unnoticed with me that he didn't answer my question. "Hampton."

"We shouldn't talk this long. If there isn't anything else..."

"Did you know?"

"Robyn, this is not the time. You know your father worked on the case. No one ever found out who shot Mancini. That is still the truth."

"I'll talk to you later."

"Are you sure everything's okay?"

"Yes, I'm fine. Just do what I said, please."

There's only one way to distract Kendall from the inevitable revelations: I have to give her some revelations on my own. I already caught Jimmy talking to Arturo when officially no one knows where he is—a fact that is connected to the list, Fiori's death, and once again, that evening.

Maybe it's true that he's investigating on Kendall's behalf. It would be helpful if I could sow just a little more doubt and discord between the two.

It might be sheer dumb luck, but the moment arrives when he once again walks into Kendall's office and sits behind the computer. Not long after that, he gets a phone call and hurries to leave. I notice he left his jacket on the chair and have a hard time not rolling my eyes.

This is the most stressful moment yet. I wait until Sue leaves her desk for a moment, then head over there and open her drawer to retrieve her key card. Again, my heart is beating in my throat when I'm in Kendall's office, going through the pockets of Jimmy's coat. I retrieve a crumbled piece of paper. The screen of the desk top computer is still set to the bank website, but of course I can't get in now.

I smooth the paper and can't help smiling at the numbers I see. If this means what I think it does, my hopes have just come true.

Chapter Sixteen

Jess heads to her apartment for an errand, and I can't stall any longer. When Jimmy comes into my office, as usual with coffee and treats, I gesture for him to sit. I'll get the truth out of him. Now. There are already people I trust more than him, Cousin Luca, Jess, and either one might appreciate being elevated into this position.

It's not like Jimmy playing the old-fashioned role he had at my dad's side has a lot of advantages for me. I don't need anyone to beat people up for me. I need someone loyal, who understands money, secrets, and the necessity to bend the rules sometimes. I doubt that he's still that person.

"What are you thinking about?" he asks.

"Many things. Arturo, for example. I wonder why he split, and where he might be."

He doesn't even blink. "Who knows? It's not like we need him."

"Perhaps, but I was surprised to learn that apparently, you know."

Realization dawns on his face, quickly giving way to anger.

"You believe her over me? You want to insult me, Kendall?"

"I don't think you can call that an insult. You are talking to Arturo. I defended you in front of her, damn it!" I don't need to raise my voice much to make him realize I'm just as angry. "I can't have this from you. Jessica is in my life now. I suggest you get over it, or you get out."

"I don't have a problem with her as long as you keep your head straight. You want to find out who killed your dad. Arturo might be able to help us get a lead on that Blake Ford, but he got into some bad shit with Bianco and is hiding from him."

Another pissing contest between two guys, how precious. I shake my head.

"What were you thinking, keeping something like this from me?"

"I wasn't going to keep it from you forever. This is not how Alphonso and I worked together. I don't understand why you can't trust me."

Oh no. I can't deal with his hurt feelings on top of everything.

"Tell me exactly what he said to you. I might be able to trust you again. Besides, you know how I work. You've known for a while now, and you never complained."

"It's been difficult. The Biancos are itching for a fight, and...don't get mad at me, Kendall. I know you don't want to hear this, but everyone is worried about a power vacuum, and that the Biancos might use that to take control of the city."

"All this means is that a lot of people have been lying to my mother's face, and mine. Don't make the same mistake."

"You don't want to lose me."

"Say that again? Are you threatening me?"

He sighs. "Come on, you're determined to misunderstand me. I didn't tell you about Arturo yet because I wanted to wait until there's something final to report. In case you hadn't noticed, that's my job, to clear away obstacles so you can pretend that running a real estate group is all that you do. Who else do you think would be able to do it?"

A couple of people, off the top of my head. I don't want to continue this tiring conversation.

"Do your job, but report to me more frequently. If I don't have time, I will tell you. And leave Jess alone."

He shrugs. "Whatever you want."

"You're right in one thing," I say, changing tactics. "I need a friend. Not an old-fashioned concept to present to my uncles who will never listen to anything that comes out of a woman's mouth. I don't want to validate their bigotry or Bianco's. I know that you know better than that."

"I care about you, Kendall." He holds my gaze for long enough to make the moment uncomfortable.

"I value that. Let's get back to work and let me know the moment you hear from Arturo."

"Of course."

After a knock on the door, Jess walks inside. Jimmy gives her an irritated look before he leaves. This won't be over anytime soon.

"Hey. Good morning." When we are alone, I get up to greet her with a kiss.

"It was," she says wistfully.

"Is everything okay?"

"Yes. Of course. I just didn't get a lot of sleep last night." She smiles. "It's hard to think of work when you have a weekend away with a gorgeous woman planned."

"Well, a couple more workdays, and we're there. It will go by fast, I promise. You've been so good helping out Sue I'd like to take you to another site today. Luca is coming too."

"That sounds great. So, you talked to Jimmy?"

"I did. Don't worry about him. He knows better than to bother you about the phone call you overheard. Just like I assumed, he was communicating with him on behalf of the company, hasn't gotten around to telling me yet."

"Okay then. I suppose we have some work to do now?"

⁓ℓℓ⁓

Jimmy thinks I'm careless, not thinking with my brain, but that couldn't be further from the truth. Not everyone who married into the Mancini family was introduced to all aspects of the business right away, though when they took their vows, they knew they'd have to learn, and prove themselves.

Jess and I haven't addressed the future much. I think it's not too early to give her a glimpse of the possibilities. It would make my job, and my life in general, easier. She, Luca and Jimmy could share responsibilities for a while—in any scenario it would be much more attractive than trying to get that tiny business off the ground. If design matters to her this much, she could still work at it.

There'll be a lot to talk about at the cabin. Jess doesn't know it yet, but I've made arrangements to stay longer than the weekend. Jimmy has orders to check in. Everything will be perfect.

We head to the site in the afternoon, meeting with contractors for another new development. I introduce Jess to the project manager.

"For now, Jessica works for my assistant, but she's interested in all aspects of the business."

He looks surprised but doesn't question my judgment. Thank God, I needed that today. Luca smiles, apparently one of the few men in my family who gets it. His wife is an accountant. She quit her firm and has worked for us ever since. We are always grateful to add talent wherever possible.

"I'm a designer," Jess says. "I have my own firm."

"And I think we'll soon use her services," Luca confirms. We tour the site with the project manager, and I'm proud to see Jess engage with him.

Mom and Dad would have loved her. This project started when my mother was still alive, and her friendship with the mayor helped secure the contract. We'll see it through—just like the search for Blake Ford. The more I involve other people, the easier it will be to keep Jimmy at arm's length, which is the best solution now that we are at a standoff. What he wants will never happen.

Chapter Seventeen

When we get back to headquarters, Kendall heads to a meeting, and I use the time for a quick visit to the restroom. I wash my hands lost in thought. Hampton is capable, and I have no doubt he did the right thing. I'm pondering what I saw today, too, Kendall taking me to that construction site. It's one thing to read about the numbers of the Mancini Group, another to see those numbers in action. It's impressive, and brazen.

I dry my hands, startled when the door opens and Jimmy Bruno walks in.

"Hey. I don't think...What the hell are you doing?"

He's locking the door, and the next moment my back is against the wall, his hand clamping over my throat. Within seconds, it's getting hard to breathe. Only when I'm starting to see stars, he lets go of me. I slump against the wall.

"Are you insane?"

"Who are you?" He's so close he almost spits in my face.

"You know who I am, and you're jealous! Kendall will not tolerate this!"

"Kendall isn't here now, is she? Besides, she'll be happy to find out who she can really trust."

I shake my head, wince, my hand going to my neck. I can feel the bruise forming.

"What do you want? Kendall knows she can trust me. You, I'm not so sure. You're keeping a lot of secrets from her, considering the position you have. I didn't ask her for anything. Why are you in my face?" My voice sounds hoarse.

"Because I look out for her. I have since she was a teenager, and I can smell it if something's not right. Cute, innocent Jess, that's not you."

"I was right. You *are* insane."

"And you are not who you say you are. I'll give you a chance, though, if by this weekend, you break up with her."

"What?"

"You heard me. You're distracting her, and that's dangerous in ways you can't even imagine." He steps closer to me once more, and I flinch. I'd love to kick him in a painful place, but unfortunately, I'll have to be "cute, innocent" Jess for a little while longer.

"What if I don't do it?"

"I'd do anything to protect her. I can make your life hell in more ways than you can imagine."

"Let me go," I demand.

"You have until Friday night. If you tell her about this, I promise you things will get worse."

Fuck you.

This is bad. I thought I had the weekend to talk to her about her options. I need to make it quick, and efficient.

"If I tell her, you'll be out of a job. But I won't. I'm giving you one more chance."

I walk to the door with my head held high and my heart racing, but he doesn't try to stop me.

I didn't expect this. I barely had my initiation. I'll have to move faster to end this fever dream, remind myself that I don't owe her anything. A part of me still prays she wouldn't be okay with what just happened.

—ℓℓ—

Kendall is blissfully oblivious to the scene that just unfolded, but she won't be for much longer. Since the timetable has moved up, there's no reason to hold anything back, at least where Jimmy is concerned.

I walk right back to her office.

"We need to talk," I say without preamble.

Kendall gets up from behind her desk and picks up her coat and purse.

"Let's go."

—ℓℓ—

She directs the driver to *Catania*. I wish this could happen any other place, but apparently that's not my choice. We don't talk during the drive. The atmosphere is heavy, I guess both of us aware that time is running out.

"Things are getting complicated," Kendall remarks when we enter the restaurant, heading straight to "our" table in the back. The man behind the counter nods. Pretty much everyone in Kendall's world has seen and accepted, for better or worse, that we've become inseparable. Everyone but Bruno, that is.

She signals the waiter, and without further prompting, he brings the wine.

"You're telling me you don't want to go on the weekend trip?"

I take a deep breath. "No. That's not what I was going to tell you. Remember what we said about honesty?"

"It wasn't that long ago."

"I am not a designer."

Kendall shrugs it off. "I figured there had to be something else. You had the general idea, and it all sounded right, but...I had a feeling."

I knew this moment would come sooner rather than later with the speed this case has been developing. The case...and something else. I still feel a bit lightheaded. So much depends on me getting this right.

Lives might depend on it.

"You're going to tell me?" Kendall prompts. Does she really have no idea?

"I've been hired to look into Jimmy, for insurance fraud and a few other things that concern you as well." That is a little less of a lie though still vague. "It's the time to tell you so you can assess if and how your business was impacted, but I'm afraid it was. He stole from you."

No huge sums, but it's still curious enough given that he claims his absolute loyalty to her. Then again, he's the consummate macho guy, who thought he should have been rewarded with an easy in a long time ago. He won't see anything wrong with keeping these transactions from Kendall.

I study her expression which is more tired than anything. She knows him well—perhaps she suspected.

"I've been planning to make some changes. Those take time though, and in the meantime, I'm afraid I still need him."

"Are you okay with this?"

I can see her face fall when I draw aside the collar of my shirt to reveal the bruise. She reaches for her cell phone, and I lay my hand over hers.

"Not yet. I understand that you need to take action. You'll have to have your ducks in a row. Let's do this the right way."

She holds on to my hand.

"The right way?" She sounds bitter, frustrated. "Who hired you, Jess?"

"I was going to tell you everything on the weekend, but then this..." I tap the discolored skin lightly, wincing. "This happened. I want to give you some time before I have to report back to my boss. We are only interested in Bruno. And for the record...The rest was real." I might as well stop fooling myself and her. I have an interest in bringing this to an end that's acceptable for both of us, somehow.

"I'll talk to Luca. Then we can go."

"You think that's a good idea?"

"Unless you want to leave right now, and we call it quits." She sighs.

"I never met anyone like you. I'm so sorry I had to lie. I want to have that conversation with you, see where it leads us, but I understand if you couldn't leave town at the moment."

Kendall sits back, studying me in return. "You lied to me. Jimmy lied to me too, but the difference is, I swore to myself I'd never accept shit like that from anyone. My parents didn't run things like this. When Sofia Bianco knocked on their door, they took her in. To be honest, I've been frustrated with Jimmy for a while. I know he thinks he deserves a promotion, and maybe that was true at some point, but this is too much."

"I understand, but is this going to work out? Does he have friends in the company?"

"Only as long as I say so. Neither Luca nor Uncle Lorenzo will tolerate this kind of behavior. We say he's out, he's out."

"I'm so sorry about all this."

"It's been a long time coming."

"No, I mean..."

"I know what you mean. Let me do this, and we can figure out the rest."

Best case scenario—Kendall will be more motivated than ever to contain Bruno, something we can help her with if she helps us, with him and the Biancos. Which means she might let up on trying to find Blake Ford. It's a win-win situation, right?

I am tired too.

"I'm going to call Luca," Kendall says. "Then we'll eat."

It seems premature, but I'm feeling relieved when we have a meal on the table twenty minutes later. I showed her the number of the offshore account on the piece of paper I got out of Jimmy's coat, and the connections I've made thanks to my colleagues. Money going into an offshore account on a regular basis—an account in his name, and those sums have nothing to do with the Mancini Group.

Kendall has been taking the revelations in stride.

"I've never been good at delegating," she says with a shrug. I still admire her flexibility in dealing with a host of new situations. She's likely been doing it constantly for the past few years. "I guess it's something I need to learn, and Luca and Claudia are more than ready to step in. Everyone got too used to leaning on Jimmy all the time."

"What's going to happen to him?"

"He'll be out with a final pay, and his access to business accounts will be denied. We have a protocol in place. Luca can handle the rest, and besides, we'll be back on Monday."

"This is quick. You had time to look at what I gave you?"

"Enough," she says grimly. "But unless you tried to strangle yourself, I didn't need a lot of numbers. Everyone agrees, this is a red line."

It's interesting and refreshing that a family that is involved in all sorts of shady operations will not tolerate domestic and otherwise violence against women. Clearly a point to make for women in power everywhere, even when it comes to criminal enterprises. It might be the wine, or the adrenaline that makes me giddy.

"You are amazing," I say.

"I appreciate the flattery, but I'll still want details from you. You're a private investigator I assume?"

"Something like that. I normally draw a line between investigations and my private life...I didn't mean to lead you on for the sake of information." I'm walking a fine, dangerous line here. I need to string her along for a little while longer, and at the same time I know I'm hooked.

"I took the risk. You're coming home with me?"

"If you want me to..."

"I don't think you should be alone tonight. And I don't want to be." Her tone, now warm and seductive, sends a shiver down my spine. Whatever happens with Bruno, hell, whatever happens this weekend, I want a few more hours of reprieve, the only thing that's ever been real for us.

"I know it's complicated right now, but I like where this is going."

"Good. I'll have someone pack up dessert."

I'm in a different reality, at a safe distance from all possible complications in Kendall's condo, in her bed.

I still haven't figured out if she's feeling so self-assured, lonely, or guilty, that she's decided all the answers can wait another day—because I haven't given her much in that regard.

Perhaps it's all right because I'm giving her my body instead. Bliss has taken me over as she's administering a sensual massage. The lights are dimmed. I might be falling asleep before anything else happens, but when she kisses my neck, her hand sliding between my thighs, my body wakes with a start. Kendall smiles at my gasp.

Perhaps this isn't just for me. I'm aware that her frustration with Bruno has been rising for some time. Just imagining that we're here together will make him mad, and that might be a stray thought on her mind. Not that I have any reason to complain, not at all.

"I can handle little lies," she whispers. "I always keep the big picture in mind."

"I'm...glad." It's hard to focus on anything besides her warm, gentle touch.

"I want you in my life. Whatever they're paying you, I can pay you more."

The words linger on my mind even when my body revels in perfect pleasure. I'm not sure she's talking about Jess, the private investigator, at this point.

Sometime soon, we'll have to start negotiating for real.

In light of the previous day's events, Kendall wants me to stay away from headquarters. She'll go up to the cabin to prepare things, and a driver will pick me up around six. I don't like being away from it all for this long. There's no denying I have some prep work to do, which is more than to pack for a weekend away.

I finally call Hampton.

"Bruno is out?" he says. "Wow. How did you do that?"

"Wasn't all that hard. Look..." This is the tricky part. I'm in no position to negotiate a deal of any kind, but I have to make sure Kendall has an incentive to work with us. Otherwise...No. It would always be better. "I'm sure she's going to deliver some big names. I'm close. We have some things on Bruno, but it would be good to know if the DA would be...flexible when it comes to Kendall."

114

"Why would they be?" he asks, sounding confused. "She declared a vendetta against the person who shot her father. For starters."

"Yes, but she has a lot of other things on her mind now. She's frustrated with Bruno, and some of her family members. She'll help us, I'm sure. All I need is a bit more time to convince her. Having a good reason, like a more lenient sentence, would help."

"There will be time for that. For now, you need to finish what you started."

That's easier said than done. I'm relieved he doesn't know all of it.

"And Robyn, there's someone here who wants to talk to you."

"Hampton, wait a second—"

"Hello, Robyn."

I freeze. This is all wrong.

"Dad! Why are you there? Did something happen?"

"No, we're all fine."

I can't help the relieved sigh, though I'm still all jittery inside.

"What's going on?"

"I think there's a misunderstanding that I can help clear up. I guess by now you know I didn't just help prep the case against Alphonso. I was there, and my name was kept off the list for a reason. He and I had known each other for a long time. We went to school together."

"Wait. What? Why didn't I know about this?"

"We all thought it was better to keep it under wraps, for everyone's safety. Yours and Mom's in the first place."

A cold shiver runs down my spine.

"You didn't shoot Alphonso Mancini, did you?"

"No, I didn't. Kendall should know that. But I was deep undercover at the time."

I don't know what to think or say. "This could have helped me."

"I know, and I'm sorry. Hampton came to talk to me about a security detail, and that's when I decided you should know the truth. Al and I were close friends at some point, and that gave me an in. To be honest, I thought I could make a difference for him. The longer I stayed, the more I believed he might want to change..."

"Dad, what is this really about?"

"Don't get carried away. They're friendly, and they have some surprising standards."

"Sofia Bianco."

"Yes. But that doesn't negate everything else that's going on. There's still a lot of unaccounted money going around. People disappear."

"Come on. This is not my first case."

"I know it isn't. But the Mancini family is a special case."

"I'm aware," I say, feeling defensive and silly all at once. It's not like he's telling me anything new, is he? "You be careful, but don't worry about me. I know how to do my job. I have to go."

I'm not lying for once, because there's a knock on the door. I put the phone back in its hiding place and go to answer.

Chapter Eighteen

B y noon, I have about two dozen text messages and missed calls from Jimmy. During the day, I can see that he's slowly giving up, which is fine with me as I'm having lunch with Luca and Claudia at Adria.

Taking action is calming, though not enough to chase the restless antsy feeling from my body. The double espresso at the end of the meal brings it back in full force.

This isn't over yet. I can't even be sure that Jimmy did a thorough job on Jess's background. I ask Claudia to follow up while Luca has been dealing with Jimmy.

"He's pissed," Luca says when my phone is vibrating again.

"Pissed enough to do something stupid?"

Like, go to the police?

"I could convince him not to, though he thinks you owe him an explanation in person."

"He wants an explanation?" I shake my head. "He attacked Jessica, in the women's restroom at headquarters. I don't have to give him any more of an explanation, but if he insists, how about stealing from the family? If Dad had known, he'd have kicked him out on his ass much sooner."

"I'm sure," Luca says. "He didn't steal during those days, because he was still hoping you'd marry him."

"Stop it. Not you too."

"I'm not going to say anything...other than, I've always admired you for standing up to the less evolved members of our family."

"Thanks, I guess. I was never going to marry him, even if I was straight."

"Yeah, you were lucky, too. Al and Angela had views very different from my father."

Various implications hang in the air for a moment. It's not a good time to follow up on them.

"We were all lucky to have them in our lives when we did. All right. I have work to do. Just make sure Jimmy doesn't act out, okay?"

He nods. "I'll keep an eye on him."

Maybe I'm crazy, but I still hope we can figure this out somehow. Jess could have given the information to her boss and run, but she didn't. In fact, she's at her apartment, getting ready for our weekend away.

I still want to fulfill my duties to my family, the promise to my mother.

More than ever before, I've realized during the past few weeks that I also want what they had. My mother didn't come from a connected family, so she didn't know details in the beginning. They were in love. They decided that this was what mattered most to them, up until death first separated, and then reunited them.

It's rare, it's not promised, but what if it exists for me, too? I'll press Jess for answers in a place where she'll have nowhere to go. If I don't forgive her for these little white lies, I might never know who she could be in my life.

Time flies when you have a business to run. I'm about to leave my office when both Luca and Claudia come inside. They both look serious, and my first thought is that Jimmy went off the rails.

"You should sit down," Luca says.

"Is it Jimmy? What the hell did he do?" I keep standing.

"We can't reach Jimmy," Claudia says, "but we think he might be laying low, drowning his sorrows somewhere. This is about Jessica Byrne, better known as Robyn Johnson."

A different name, does it still count as white lie?

"She's FBI," Luca adds. "They tried to get to Al that way, now they're pulling the same thing. I'm sorry, Kendall."

They're my family, but they're also expecting leadership from me, which is even more important since Jimmy is out. What he did remains the same even given this new information.

"That changes things slightly, but we have to keep an eye out on Jimmy. If he wants to talk to me, I'll see him on Monday to inform him on the error of his ways. I'd still like to take Ms. Johnson out to the cabin."

I can tell from their expressions that they don't like what I'm saying.

"You have to be careful," Luca warns.

"Why? I'll just have a conversation with her. You'll make sure that everything stays calm around here...with Bruno, and her colleagues. Can you do that for me?"

"Yes, of course," he says quickly.

"I'm not changing my mind where he is concerned. I ran the numbers, and Jessica—Robyn—didn't make them up. He had no reason to attack her either."

"We'll have your back, Kendall," Claudia promises. "Whatever you need."

"Good. If you'll excuse me now...I have to go on a weekend getaway."

She doesn't know yet I'm on to her. Right on schedule, I receive the text message from the driver. They're on their way to the cabin.

It's not like I have to do a lot—staff has prepared the bedrooms and stocked the fridge. I meant to impress her. Jessica. Robyn. The FBI agent.

I'm driving too fast, not nearly as calm as I pretended to be in front of my cousins. For a split-second, I think, how stupid, and would I really mind if the car went off the road?

I grip the steering wheel tighter, steeling myself. This is not, was never about me. At least, not just about me. I still have an enormously successful business, in which Jimmy's little grab for money and power didn't make any dent.

I have my allegiances. The Biancos routinely pay off cops. We've had investigators look the other way before, and I could tell that Robyn was just the tiniest bit impressed by the luxury I can offer her. That part was not a lie.

Everyone has a price, and I'm determined to find out hers. To keep her out of my business, to keep her with me a bit longer. I might just be pathetic enough for the latter. She owes me answers. I'll make sure I'll get them. If she's FBI, she might be able to give me the name behind Blake Ford. All's well that ends well, right?

I want to cry, but once again dismiss and suppress the impulse. Whatever they throw at me, I am not weak. My parents didn't raise a naïve damsel in distress, waiting to be rescued.

Jimmy had to learn that.

Robyn will, too.

Eventually, I slow down, unwilling to get a ticket. It's gotten dark, and the nighttime driving relaxes me a bit. I'm not going to yell or pull a gun on her. Wine, food, sex, I want to mellow her down before we have that conversation. If she helps me keep my promise, maybe the story isn't over.

Naïve? We'll see.

The cabin is dark when I arrive. That's all right with me. I'm ready.

...or so I thought.

I wasn't ready for the sight that presents itself to me when I unlock the door and walk inside.

He's not supposed to be in here. Where the hell was security?

"Jimmy, how did you get in here?"

"Kendall, please, you need to hear me out!"

He holds up his hands as I train my weapon on him. It was a good idea not to come unarmed. This place has a state-of-the-art security system, and supposedly guards watching the entrances. What did he do?

"I don't have to do anything you tell me. I know that you stole from me, worse, what you did to Jess. And I know that Luca explained all of this to you already, so you can either get lost, or I'll call someone to escort you out."

He knows what that means, too. I don't have the time or patience to indulge him. I have so much more important things to think about.

Jimmy doesn't move.

"You don't want to do that," he says, his tone pleading. "We are so close to finding out who killed Alphonso. Where Jessica is concerned, I'm afraid there's bad news we have to address immediately. That's why I'm here. I'm on your side."

"What bad news? That she's with the FBI? She'll be here any minute. I'm taking care of it."

He smiles, slowly letting his arms fall to his side.

"See, Kendall, that's why you have me. The problem is already contained. I brought you a surprise."

"What the hell are you talking about?"

"Come with me, and please, don't shoot. I swear, everything is going to be fine."

He turns his back to me, and I follow him, my hand still on my gun.

Can I let him go like that? What's the alternative? The authorities—the same that got my father killed? I don't want blood on my hands. I still hope I can convince him to leave peacefully. Shutting him out of the family seems appropriate punishment for his behavior.

In the other room, he turns on a light, and, with a triumphant smile, points to the floor.

The pained whimper chills me to the bone. There's a person, hands and feet tied with a cable. A sack obscures their face, but I've seen enough.

"Are you insane? How is this helping? God, you're such an idiot." The words don't even begin to scratch the surface. I'm furious and scared at the same time. This changes everything, for all of us. What did he do?

I sink to my knees next to her, start to gently remove the sack.

"Insult me if you want, Kendall, that doesn't change the truth."

"What did you do?"

He must have caught something in my tone because he hurries to say, almost offended, "What do you think? I did what I had to do. Don't worry, I wouldn't touch a rat."

I ignore the implied accusation because he has no talking room here. Fuck no.

"I love you," Jimmy is brazen enough to add. "I'd do anything for you."

"Is that so? You can do something for me now. Get the hell out of my house and never show your face again. This proves I could never trust you."

"Kendall, do you understand what this means?"

I point the gun at him again, and this time, he gets the message and leaves. I'll deal with him later, in the right fashion.

I work as carefully as I can, still, she flinches hard under my touch. I can't help thinking that in some way, I did this, by indulging Jimmy far too long. But she'll be okay. She has to be. Jess. Robyn. At the moment, it doesn't matter.

"Relax. I got you. He's gone." I whisper nonsensical words, for her comfort or mine, I'm not sure. With the knife from my purse, I cut through the cable that binds her wrists and ankles. She blinks, as if confused.

"Don't move. I want to make sure you're okay first." Insane doesn't even begin to describe it. There's a bruise on her temple, and a cut on her lip hasn't stopped bleeding, and that's just above the clothes.

"I am so, so sorry. He's going to pay for this," I promise. I've made a lot of promises lately. I seem to have trouble keeping them.

I know that we have lawyers and a doctor on standby. The latter, I never needed in an emergency. I wonder if I should call him, and how soon he could be here.

"You'll be okay. Let's get you somewhere more comfortable."

The corners of her mouth twitch into something akin to a smile. Perhaps she's thinking about how I made her comfortable the previous night—but when I help her into a sitting position, the water shoots to her eyes.

"Sorry," I mumble. I should have shot him on the spot, jealous, petty small man. I'll make sure he's done in this city, and beyond.

"You think you can stand?"

She nods, and slowly, painstakingly, we get her to her feet. She leans hard on me. I should probably be thinking of all the disastrous consequences Jimmy's madness might have for me, but I couldn't care less. I couldn't care less that Robyn, the agent, lied to me. I half carry her to the bedroom.

"It's going to be dirty," she protests.

"Not that dirty. You're okay." I let her down as gently as possible. "I'll be right back."

I hurry as fast as I can, gather towels, Band-Aids and whatever else seems to make sense from the bathroom. She'd probably be more comfortable in PJs, but I don't know what happened to her luggage, so I take a shirt from my own suitcase.

When I come back to the room, I nearly drop the items I'm carrying. She's sitting up, biting her lip as she sets her feet on the floor. A curse escapes her lips.

Yesterday, the world was complicated, I think. Today it's impossible.

"No. You're not going anywhere...Robyn."

"You're going to do...what? Have me killed? Or beaten up?"

"You know that wasn't me. I planned to come here with you to talk. The driver..."

She shakes her head. "He was in on it."

I sit down next to her, stunned and once again wishing I could drop everything and everyone. All the time and money I invested in people, they sure haven't done a great job paying me back, or showing me any respect.

"Okay. We'll take care of all of that, but first let me take care of you. Do you need the ER?"

"Why, you have a hospital in your pocket too? Of course, you do. No."

"Are you sure? I could bring you there right now...or get someone here."

"I don't need a doctor, Kendall," she hisses, and winces.

"All right. Then let's clean you up, get you into fresh clothes and we can eat something?"

"You're delusional," she says, disbelief coloring her tone. "What do you think is going to happen?"

"What do you mean? I'll let Luca know what happened. No one in my family would sign off on this. Jimmy is out. I told you yesterday."

"Luca was with him," she says.

I'm not sure I can stand to hear anything else.

It's nothing compared to what she went through. Damn it. Damn them. I won't let them all ruin the business and reputation that my great-grandparents built.

"Let's take care of you first," I insist.

She obliges and lets me help her undress. I get the full picture of what the fight must have looked like, gritting my teeth almost as much as she is.

I keep failing everyone that matters to me.

Naïve, maybe, that my obligations are to dead people and the person who infiltrated my life in order to come up with enough evidence to arrest me. I doubt that's going to happen though it probably was Robyn's intention.

"I have some Tylenol here. I'll get you some water, and then, perhaps something to eat?"

"Stop it," she says. "Stop it already."

I lean forward to carefully embrace her. "We still need to talk. When you're feeling better."

"People are going to be worried if I don't check in on Monday."

"We'll talk about it later. Try to rest a bit. I'll be right back."

In the kitchen, I lean against the counter for a moment, surrounded by silence except for my racing heart. I can't keep trying to work with people who have too much of their own agenda. That leadership they thought was missing, perhaps they had a point. I'll show them leadership. I'm not sure they'll like it, but they had their chance.

Chapter
Nineteen

We're in trouble, there's no denying that, but I guess things could be worse. I don't know if I'm in shock, or denial. At least I'm not dead. I could easily be, though I guess Bruno was serious when he said his intention was to provide Kendall with a bargaining chip.

He was mad, so mad, because he still considers me the main obstacle to a happy marriage with her. Surely, if I didn't exist, she'd fall head over heels for a man, let alone an abusive one? I feel my throat go tight, and it's not just because of the past twenty-four hours.

How can I still have feelings for her?

Kendall returns with a tray full of amazing looking food. Less than an hour ago my fate was unclear, and perhaps it still is. I'm shocked that I got caught off guard like that, proof that falling for your target makes you careless. I had so many ideas about how to approach this weekend that I made a mistake, and it was nearly fatal.

"Don't beat yourself up," she says and cringes a bit. "I mean he's been around for years. I don't think my parents suspected anything. They'd have kicked him out long ago."

"Soup and sandwiches?" She freaking took the time to cut off the crust.

"I think we both need something comforting. I can wait until tomorrow, but as soon as you're up to it, we have to come up with some sort of game plan."

Within a heartbeat, I'm no longer sure which one of us is in denial—or shock. As it is, I'm still on assignment, and the time is now or never.

"I wish we could have done this without the drama, but we might have to act sooner than later. There is an option. You come with me on Monday, turn yourself in and you come clean. With everything. This doesn't have to end in a catastrophe for you. Jimmy, and your family, I've seen how they treat you. You don't owe them. You could finally have peace."

She looks back at me in surprise, laughs a little.

"I don't know what to say."

"Say yes. I can help you."

"I can't do that," she says patiently. "I'm running a billion-dollar company. My family...yes, they haven't always been stellar in their support, but I can't imagine doing that, ever. I have a suggestion for you, though."

"I guess there's no harm in hearing you out."

"I could get you out of the country by tomorrow. I have a good amount of property where there's no extradition treaty, and you could work for me. We forget about the rest. Jimmy is still out, of course, and I'll have someone keep an eye on him."

"Wow."

"That's all you have to say? I'm offering you an out. I promise you if Jimmy ever comes near you again, I'll shoot him. I don't care. And Luca's going to hear from me."

"Kendall. My colleagues already have a ton of evidence. Not all of it is about Bruno, but if we work together..."

"You think I'm completely naïve, don't you?"

I'm not sure how to answer. "You've been running the company for years now. I don't think someone who's

128

completely naïve could do that. But you're trying to fit into a mold that others have created for you. You can do more than that."

The spoon slips from my fingers as pain shoots up my arm. The sound it makes against the bowl startles both of us.

"Those pain pills will kick in soon. Would you care for a drink? I know I could use one. Look, I know they probably teach you these things at Quantico, and you're good at it. But my allegiance is not to Luca or Uncle Lorenzo in the first place. It's to my great-grandparents who came here with nothing and managed to buy a house they renovated, to eventually start *Catania*. My grandparents and parents who built on that. I'm not a traitor."

This is going to be more difficult than I thought, though I should probably be grateful we're having a conversation rather than a shootout. I think of Dad's words, minutes before Bruno entered my apartment. *Don't get carried away.*

"Your parents loved you. I can tell from everything you told me about them, and they thought you were the best person to lead the business. Don't you think they'd want you to do the right thing? Like they did when Sofia came to them for help?"

"There's a big difference between helping an abused woman and ratting out your whole family. No. I'm sorry, Robyn, but this isn't going to work. You have to let me do things my way. Meanwhile, I promise I'll protect you, and you can stay here as long as you want."

"You don't understand! If Jimmy turns on you, and maybe one or two people in your family, that's the end of it. Then I won't be able to help you."

"That won't happen. Don't worry."

I am hurting, frustrated and afraid, irrationally more for her than for me. At some point Bruno will realize that no matter what he lays at her feet, Kendall isn't interested in him, as a partner of any kind. I need her to testify before that sinks in. And even then...Hampton wasn't willing to make promises.

Kendall grew up in this family. I'm sure she has an idea of her chances.

"What if I could get you complete immunity?"

"Who's naïve now? Come on, we both know that's not going to happen. I'm not denying that I bent the rules on occasion. Unlike the Biancos, we don't have people killed, but we've been...let's say, creative."

"That's my point. Our objective is to prevent more bloodshed. We know that Tony Bianco would love nothing more than an all-out war he could blame on you. More chaos, more deaths. Those in your own family who already doubt your position would feel even more justified doing so."

She leans forward, her lips brushing mine in a soft kiss, halting the flow of words. I take a moment to consider how wrong this is. I could take her in right now.

It might be risky, with security and family probably nearby. The timing has to be right. At least that's what I'm telling myself.

"Tony Bianco can kiss my ass," she says, her crude words a stark contrast to the tender gesture. "He denies having anything to do with my father's death, even gave me the name of somebody who could be involved. There's something I need to do first, and that will go a long way towards clearing up this mess."

"Did it ever occur to you that it might have been a tragic accident? The lights went out, someone panicked and started shooting?"

"There was a raid. Someone ratted them out. Someone, I hear, might have been close with my family in the past. They must have had a contact."

"I didn't."

"No, all you had to do was fool poor lonely Kendall."

"I didn't say—"

"You didn't have to," she says with a sigh. "I appreciate what you're trying to do, I swear. You can't protect me from everything. I don't regret what we did, but I won't go to prison. There's too much I need to take care of now, and..." She laughs wistfully, continues, "Give up all that money? I don't think so. Sleep on it. I can do a whole lot more for you than vice versa."

It occurs to me when she made me that offer the other night, she might have suspected something.

It's still unclear to me how Bruno and Luca found out.

Chapter Twenty

I slip out of the bedroom when she's asleep. Just to be on the safe side, I check the window, and lock the door before I summon Luca. As I've predicted, he's not far, and I check in with security to let him through.

"I suppose you have something to say for yourself." I'm not going to waste my energy by yelling at him. I'll have to screen him, to figure out if he's still useful, or if he's gone off the deep end with Jimmy. "I didn't think you and Jimmy were best buddies."

"Kendall, I'm so sorry. I had no choice."

"To beat a woman? Or watch? Poor you. You know, nothing has changed regarding Jimmy, but I think I was wrong considering you for anything more important. God, my parents would be so disgusted. I know I am."

"I already said I'm sorry, but did you ever consider that your parents and mine saw things differently? I'm not proud of what I did."

"Good. You shouldn't be."

"I overheard many conversations between your father and mine. I know the way they talked—"

I hold up a hand to stop him. "No, you don't get to turn this around."

"He wanted you to marry Jimmy and have him involved in more of the business."

"You're lying to my face. That's bold."

"I'm not lying. Look, we're in the same boat, somewhat. But whatever your dad said behind closed doors, he loved you anyway. I don't have that luxury. Bruno threatened to go to Dad, and if that happened, my life would be over."

"What the hell are you talking about?"

"Alphonso might have turned a blind eye. My Dad wouldn't. He's going to kick me out on the street with nothing if he finds out."

I can feel my jaw drop. Not that I have any more sympathy for his role in tonight's insanity.

"That's just stupid. Why didn't you come to me? Does Elena know?"

He nods. "The thing is, you don't have as much power as you think you do. Everyone is content to let you handle the legitimate business because you're good at it. It makes everyone money. When it comes to the old-fashioned connections, people like my father have bypassed you, and Angela before. I'm sorry if that's all news to you. As for stupid, that's a bit mean, considering that you're harboring the FBI agent that infiltrated your family."

"So, your end game was to do what, kill her?"

"Jimmy, whatever his flaws are, and he sure has a lot of them, he loves you. He was ready to take the heat. I'm not saying this was ever a good idea, okay? I just didn't know what to do. I don't want to argue with you. I'll back you up, whatever it is you want to do."

Flaws. I saw the bruises. Luca better understands that he has a lot to make up to me. Jimmy's come crawling back several times, and his ideas of a fix were worse every time.

At this point, I want to drink myself into oblivion. I want to fall asleep and never wake up. All the work I've poured into the family business, and the family, it all seems for nothing, built on a lie. The stories people tell me about my parents are starting to sound too much alike.

"Good to know. I hope you realize that you're not doing me a favor. You don't want me to kick you out on your ass. As for now, I'm still the one you answer to, and your father does too.

"I understand."

"First thing, I want to know what Jimmy found out about the raid where my father was killed, and a man named Blake Ford. Take security with you in case he doesn't give it to you freely, and don't worry about Lorenzo. He might think he's the one in charge. He's not. I can limit his access to accounts just as easily."

"I'll remember that."

"Can you handle that?"

"I'll be fine."

"Okay. Go."

When he's gone, I take a deep breath before I pour myself another glass of wine in the kitchen, then return to the bedroom. Robyn doesn't wake up when I unlock and slip into the room.

I have no friends—not an exaggeration. I'm not sure I have any family left. I set the glass aside and lie down beside her.

I remember making love to her only days ago. Robyn. Jessica, who could have played a bigger role in the organization and my life, who could have been the one.

If I'm honest, I knew right away it was nothing but a beautiful illusion. What I'm still not sure of is why she went to these lengths. Robyn doesn't seem the type to cross lines for no reason.

We could still run away together...

But that's not a realistic option for either of us.

—ele—

The next morning, I make breakfast, as if we really had gone on a weekend getaway to take a good hard look at our relationship. Which is what we're doing, right? Kendall Mancini. Robyn Johnson. The impossible. With everything falling apart around us, sleeping next to her is still the most comforting thing that's happened to me in a while.

Immunity. Paying off a federal agent.

We've come to know each other beyond the obvious.

Robyn walks into the kitchen, looking pale and tired.

"I was going to bring you breakfast. If you need help in the shower later..."

"I'm okay," she waves off my concerns.

"I fired the driver and straightened out Luca." That seems like a weird thing to say, and her thoughtful gaze tells me that she might have caught on something I hadn't, not until now. "I'm thinking of involving Claudia more, because I think she's just as sick of all that macho bullshit. And Sofia. She's held some shares for a long time. She and my mother were good friends."

"Coffee would be good."

"Coming right up."

I sit across from her, silently praising my staff. With the fridge and pantry full, I didn't have much to do to prepare, just put everything out on the table, warm up some pre-cooked bacon in the oven. For some reason, I remember my grandmother saying how important a good breakfast was. Yesterday, neither of us had much of an appetite. I shudder at the memory of a frantic Jimmy, eager to show off.

I never meant for you to get hurt.

It would be silly to say those words. She came with an assignment. She knew the risks. It's what's on my mind regardless. While we eat, I study her. She's acting tough, which, I assume, is a habit that goes far beyond the recent experience. Having to hold her own in a man's world, it's something I can relate to.

I could make her life a lot easier if she let me, though I'm aware there could be an expiration date on that offer, just like there is on hers. I dismissed Luca's words about my limited powers, but what if I'm fighting a rising tide? I never cared much about being liked.

People don't like change, and our family had to deal with a lot, grief, my mother being pushed into a leadership position she reluctantly assumed. Then it was up to me. While I always knew I'd run the business someday, it was sooner than we all expected. Changes. Choices.

"Have you thought about it?" she asks.

"I don't think you are in a position to offer me immunity."

"I've had my colleague get in touch with the AUSA before Jimmy decided to pay me a visit. Between you not going along with whatever he'd planned, and cooperating with us, you'd be in an excellent position. And it would mean..." She gives me a wry smile. "Not all of that money would be gone. I'd assume that some of it is in places beyond my jurisdiction."

"You think? Come on, this is still a family business."

"Yeah, a few restaurants and a little real estate. You don't have to do this with me. I've studied you at work, remember?"

"It wasn't that long ago. Business and pleasure. You must think I made it too easy for you, don't you?"

She focuses on her meal for a moment, takes a sip of coffee.

"I could tell that you were different."

I can't help it, I'm laughing out loud. "No. Do better."

"It's true. I've worked in the field for some time, studied families like yours. Sure, there's rivalry, about drugs, money, territory. Most of them couldn't care less about the situation of a woman like Sofia Bianco."

"Drug trade has never been our thing. And we have standards."

"Tony and his clan, however, they're more on the traditional side. A woman gets married, she signed up for it, whatever happens. We are trying to root out the worst. I know that's not you, but you have invaluable insights. I understand that you didn't do everything by the book, but there is a path here. You're right that I can't make any definite promise, and you might not be able to avoid jail time."

"Perfect. So, let's forget about it."

"I can help you with something you want."

In that moment, it's too easy to remember how we met, started talking...She didn't run into me accidentally. Attraction, that wasn't something planned, made up.

"I think you've 'helped' enough."

"At this point, no one knows who killed your father. I swear to you I'm telling the truth. But if you really want to find out, I have access to different resources. We could work on this together."

She's so good, on every level. I can't resent her after what she's endured, from people that are supposed to have my back, but maybe I do.

"Because I have such good reasons to trust you, Agent Johnson."

I'm not above having a brief moment of satisfaction when she winces.

"I deserved that. But I'm serious. I understand this matters a lot to you."

"It does, and if you know all that, you know that I got a name. Blake Ford."

She holds my gaze for a few seconds.

"What?"

"Yes, we need to talk about that too. I thought you might know...He and your dad were childhood friends. Blake was working an undercover assignment when they reunited, and...His last name is Johnson. He's my father," she confirms when I stare at her in disbelief. "He didn't kill Alphonso, but I'm sure we can finally understand what really happened."

"Oh, wow. Runs in the family. I shouldn't be surprised."

"We can figure this out together."

"Or I could just call my lawyer and work out a strategy that will kill your case before it goes anywhere and end your career. I must admit I'm not sure how this undercover thing works, but sleeping with your target would undermine what you're trying to achieve, no?"

I don't wait for an answer. Instead, I pick up my coffee cup and leave.

There is no solution, and with every honest answer, the truth looks worse. Robyn's father. Another generation, another betrayal. Somehow, I fear that this story only can end with one of us dead. Why couldn't I stick with meaningless one-night stands? Everything is crumbling, and for the first time, I'm willing to believe it's all my fault.

Chapter Twenty-One

I 'm black and blue all over, feel it with every move. The tug of war is painful beyond the physical. I feel like I used up all my cards, but if Kendall isn't listening to me, there's a limit as to how much I can help her.

I know she locked the door to the room last night—and she's willing to protect me from the demons surrounding her. I'm not sure how long that will work for either of us. The sharks are likely to smell blood in the water already.

I wish I could talk to the AUSA right now. Between delivering Bruno, Bianco and the less friendly elements in her own family, Kendall could be safe. But reassurances and possibilities aren't enough for her.

With a sigh, I pick up another piece of bacon. I might as well take advantage. As long as the security staff and most people in the Mancini Group still answer to her, we can maintain a dubious sense of safety. Luca Mancini might have learned a lesson. I don't think Bruno has, and it's important to find out where the rest of the family will come down.

Against all odds, I think Kendall's parents had to be special to accept her within the structures of a traditional crime family. That's still what the Mancinis are.

Kendall walks back into the kitchen, looking somber as she pours herself another cup.

"Coffee got cold?" I ask. If I'm honest, I was attracted to her when I first saw her. I want to find a solution in which neither of us has to lose everything—or anything. Wishful thinking?

"Let's do it," she says. "Let's find out who killed my dad, and I'll get you something on Bianco that's enough to put him away...and the rest of them."

I nod, relieved beyond measure.

—ell—

"I need you to be honest from now on," Kendall declares. "For my sake, and so I can make sure you're safe while we do this. When were you planning to call in the cavalry? Because you would have already if you thought you had enough."

"Enough" is a relative term, but she has a point.

"I just have to give the word. I wanted to make sure..." Kendall gives me a pointed look.

"That I could have this talk with you, and what exactly would be the details. This is real. If you can help us, it's not going to be that bad."

"You keep saying that." She sounds amused. "Why does it matter to you?"

"I wish we could have met under different circumstances. You don't have to believe me, but it's true." When she doesn't affirm or deny, I continue, "I already know that you had your eyes on Rossi as well. His name was on Marina Fiori's list."

"Arturo. Yes, it's strange that Jimmy was in touch with him, but I suppose that happened while we were having our second date at *Catania*. Arturo has no problem

142

throwing his kids under the bus, and I assume that's why Carlo is now in custody."

"You don't think he murdered Fiori?"

"Maybe, maybe not. In any case, Arturo has for a long time tried to get back into Tony Bianco's good graces. Jimmy mentioned something about, I quote, 'bad shit' he got involved in." Kendall shakes her head. "It was Tony who gave me your father's name."

"To distract from himself?"

"A very obvious play, but he's not a subtle guy. It's possible."

"At that fundraiser, it's Arturo, your dad and mine. He obviously knew that the FBI was raiding the place that night, but they had very different plans. Someone else knew they were coming."

"Tony says he wasn't anywhere near, not that I trust him. I didn't recognize anyone connected to him on the list."

"What if it wasn't complete?"

Kendall sighs. "Then Marina lost her life for nothing. I can't believe after all of this we're still at square one."

"Maybe not. The weakest link...It still appears to be Carlo Rossi. If he told Jimmy where to find Arturo, he might tell my partner as well, and then we have someone who was in the room. We know he wants to please Tony. Let's see if we can work with that?"

"It's a start," she admits. "I swear I wasn't kidding about Jimmy either. I kept him around because he always was, and he helped us after my father's death. Now I realize he never listened to a thing I said."

"You're ready to turn him in?" This is important. What happened last night, I'll survive, but it will go on the record. What Kendall does with it matters, and not just because I want her to be on the right side of all of this.

"You mean I can't put out the word, so he'll be taken care of?"

It takes a moment for me to realize she's yanking my chain. "Not the time."

"I want you to know that I'd never sign up on what he did. Never."

"I understand, but the best way to show me is to eventually work with me and my colleagues. Jimmy, whatever you can give us on the Biancos, and..."

"Eventually, ratting out my own family." We both wince at the term.

"Kendall, I'm sorry about your parents. They seemed like good people. I met some of your extended family, remember? With the exception of Claudia and Sofia maybe, they were ready to marry you off to Jimmy so they could keep up appearances, have a man in charge."

I have to be careful not to get ahead of myself, but I am hurting, and more than a little frustrated. Not all of it is Kendall's fault, I know. If I hadn't been this easy, we'd be having a different conversation, and we'd unlikely be having it here.

We can't change what is real. She's still at the top of the Mancini clan, I'm the cop on the inside, and no one has fired a shot yet. There's a reason for that.

"Yes, some of them are jerks. You don't throw people in jail for being a jerk, do you?"

"No, but we do it for tax evasion, money laundering and murder. And if it was up to me, I'd prefer it be them rather than you."

"What, you wouldn't wait for me?"

"Are you taking this seriously?"

She sobers up right away.

"I am. I swear. Whatever happens after that, I promised my mother on her deathbed I would find the truth."

"I know. I heard what you said in church."

"Yes, and I haven't had much success so far."

"You did what you could while still running the company. It will be different now."

Perhaps I did get hit over the head too hard, but when I catch her gaze on me, I'm certain she's thinking, wondering the same.

What if we managed to uncover the truth?

Where would that lead either of us?

Together?

—ell—

She insists on helping me in the shower after all, and the following minutes run the range of emotions, from awkward to painful and back to strangely sensual.

I can't be this vulnerable with everything that's on the line, and I'm relieved when I'm no longer naked, but dressed in a set of fresh clothes.

The fact that they cover the bruises is a relief too.

Kendall went about her task quietly, her touch infinitely gentle. But I know those hands have held a gun, signed false declarations.

It hasn't exactly been a romantic getaway, but at the end of the weekend, we have a plan. We'll spend one more night and then go home. It will be the start of many confrontations, and all those efforts will have to shake something loose—with the Rossis, Biancos, and at work.

Are we learning anything new about each other? I'm not sure. Kendall is suspicious by nature, and she still went for everything Jessica Byrne had to offer. I knew what to expect from her. I couldn't resist.

Later in the afternoon, she brings me a glass of wine. In fact, she's been waiting on me all day, ignoring my protest.

Kendall, still looking immaculate even when all hell is about to break loose, sits next to me on the couch after handing me my glass.

"What would you do if you weren't with the FBI?" she asks. "Interior design maybe?"

"I didn't think there was much of a choice. It's what I always wanted to do. You?"

Kendall takes a sip before she answers. "There's pride in continuing a family tradition."

"Did you ever think of anything else?"

"Lately...a lot," she confesses. "But there's no point. We are who we are, right?"

"You are good at this. You could run a clean business."

"And let people like the Biancos have it all? When I said we could get out of the country and never look back, weren't you at least a little bit tempted? Think about your answer. Everyone knows a cop who has looked the other way."

"Not in my unit," I say, aware of how testy I sound. Yes, I was tempted, for a second or so. Not because of a desire to break the law and get away with it. Desire...It's complicated.

"Okay. Then you understand it's not an easy decision for me either."

That strikes me as amusing. "It's hardly the same."

"How is it different? You try to surround yourself with people you can trust...more or less."

"You might not be in the business of killing people, or running drugs, but the numbers hardly add up all the time. You paid people to look the other way. All that money disappearing into secret places, it's not like there's no victim in that."

"Maybe I find better ways to spend my money than the government."

"We're going down that road...Why don't you enlighten me then? Where is it that your money is well-spent?"

"Why don't we take a break?" she suggests, and without waiting, takes my glass from me.

"Hey. Are you sure I want to do this sober?"

"I'm sure." Kendall leans in and kisses me, her lips tasting of the sweet red wine. Even though my mind is overloaded with a long list of the necessary steps, the distraction works, better than I care to admit.

"What are you doing?"

"Something I might not be able to do, ever again, after this weekend."

She leans back, her gaze calm.

"You know I'll have to deal with Jimmy in a way that makes sure my family knows the truth. You'll check in with your people, but whatever you'll be able to cook up with the prosecutor, this, us, will likely be gone."

I can't argue with that—or my body's reaction to her suggestion.

"I'm afraid you could be right. I'm not sure I'm all that flexible yet."

"What if you let me do the work?" she asks.

It's an offer too good to refuse.

From the moment I began to study Kendall Mancini, I learned this about her: She's prone to big emotions, drama, and grand gestures. Whatever her environment might have contributed to shaping her that way, it's fascinating and irresistible to me. Something clicks between us, her, and me coming from a family context that's a lot more strict and sober.

But she's also been lonely, reflecting something back at me that I was unwilling to face before. We can pretend a little while longer.

Chapter Twenty-Two

T his is mad. We must both be mad. Jimmy and Luca have put me into this impossible situation. Perhaps I'm trying to make excuses for letting her in, but they sure have done their share. I quietly put things in motion while Robyn was asleep last night. I don't know if it will be enough until Robyn and I get back to the city.

A lot of people have certain expectations of me.

I need to act. Some would say it's suicidal to let her go back to converse with her colleagues—Lorenzo and the rest of the clan wouldn't mind getting rid of the Biancos altogether, but they're not stupid. They know that the FBI would come looking at them just the same, and if they think it's all because of me...

Before, I'd discuss strategy with Jimmy, but he turned from the reliable guy in the background into a creepy jealous stalker. Worse even, he was never that guy, buying into all that macho bullshit from the get-go. How did it get this far? How could Dad not see what was happening?

Except...No, that's not possible. Sitting up against the headboard, I almost shake my head. My parents both knew who I was, and they both planned for me to take over the business. Not Lorenzo, not Luca, not Jimmy.

Dad might have felt a bit nostalgic because Jimmy joined the organization as a teenager, but he knew that I was never going to just step aside.

There's no way he was scheming with Jimmy behind my back.

I think of everything Robyn has said, what she has promised me, that we could unravel the last strands together. Will it be enough? Will it be possible at all?

I wish I knew what to do. I lift a hand and brush it down Robyn's back, gently enough not to wake her, or so I thought.

She turns to me.

"I know it's a lot, but you'll be all right."

She doesn't know everything that's on the line, or what I need to do. But I'll do my best to protect her. One thing hasn't changed—I still don't want blood on my hands, least of all hers.

⁓ele⁓

Monday morning comes too soon—no more stalling. We are going to stop for breakfast on the way, but first I call Luca.

"What's the situation with Jimmy?"

"That's your first question? I did what you said, updated everyone on Jimmy. Not everyone is pleased, that's the situation."

"You're still worried he could out you?"

"That's done, Kendall," he says tersely. "Claudia convinced me that I had to do it."

"Oh...How did it go?"

"You're having a romantic weekend with your FBI agent, and you really want to know about that?"

"Okay, later. So, Jimmy. Is he going to be a problem? Anyone taking his side?"

"To answer both of your questions, no, I took care of it, and Dad will get over it though he wishes I was more like Jimmy."

Robyn stays in the room for this conversation. There's not much she can do with it anyway.

"All right. We are coming home. And don't worry, it's not as bad as you think. They are after the Biancos. We can help them, everyone wins."

"You're being overly optimistic, Kendall. What did she tell them?"

"Nothing you or your dad need to worry about. Let's have a family meeting at my place tonight, just us, Elena, Claudia and Marc, and your parents. We'll figure something out."

"I'll pass it on," he says, not sounding much convinced.

"I'm serious. This will go away. They don't want to spend endless resources on us when they can get to the real boogeyman."

"Tony Bianco? Why don't they have someone on the inside with him?"

"Luca, come on. Why do you think so many of them went into the witness protection program?"

That might be an urban legend, but it shuts him up for the moment.

"Tell Lorenzo everything is under control, and I'll see him later."

"Yes, Ma'am."

When I end the call, Robyn says, "That's not really what we agreed on."

"I know. You understand that until I've taken the temperature in the room, I can't tell anyone what we agreed on, right?"

"Right," she agrees. "Let's go. I'm starving."

I don't usually have meals at roadside diners, but now that we're both kind of undercover, it seems to fit. I can't help wondering if we ever had a chance to look beyond all the layers.

Intimacy was a pleasant and dangerous way to go beyond the fixed roles, but there's bound to be more. Everyday life. The private side of Agent Johnson. Against all odds, I'm still curious about her. All in good time. We'll go check on her apartment, and later meet with the family.

The in between is still tricky. She wants to go meet with her team and the prosecutor. It's not a good time for that yet. I have to convince her that we can find Arturo and lean on him a bit harder without involving the FBI yet.

Everything else, Tony, and any deals, can wait. Robyn might not see it that way, but it's the best for all of us.

"What are you thinking?" she asks, spreading honey onto her toast with a knife.

"It will be strange to finally have confirmation." It's not exactly a lie. "After my mother's death, all I could think about was to fulfill her wish. Even you tell me it's a mystery, but I guess Tony pointing fingers at your dad is a big clue. Then it will be over and...I'm not sure what's left."

"There will still be a business."

"Yes, there might be."

It's inconvenient that she got her hands on some of those numbers. It's not the worst. My financial well-being and future are secure. Otherwise...I don't know. I'm not sure what I'll have to do or buy to stop grieving for the people I cared about—or to start doing so.

Mom, Dad...and Jess Byrne.

We arrive at her—Jess's apartment—close to ten a.m. It makes me wonder how Robyn lives. I have an idea of what she makes, but that can be relative.

She's not new to town. An assignment like hers would take months to prepare, and there's the story of her father...That still boggles the mind. Blake. Alphonso. The irony of it all.

We go up in the elevator, and I'm thinking about how to break it to her that she'll need to stay with me for at least another couple of days. There can't be any contact with her colleagues in that time, or I won't be able to protect her, or myself.

There's not much time.

Robyn unlocks the door, her posture tense. "Wait here."

"Why? Do you think—?"

"I don't think anything. Just wait. I'll be right out."

"Okay. Just remember I made that call in front of you."

She gives me a wry smile. "I'm not going to call anyone now," she says and walks inside. It's a bit funny, because I don't usually let other people tell me what to do, let alone an FBI agent trying to dismantle my business. Well, that's perhaps taking it a bit far, but still. Lost in thought, I turn around to come face to face with a nightmare, a figure dressed in black carrying a rifle. A freaking rifle.

"Tell Tony that he needs to fucking talk to me if he wants something." I'm angry. Livid. Most of all, I can't acknowledge any fear, not even in this situation. Just like I could never live the full extent of my grief. It's tiring.

I move my hand an inch, and he grips the weapon tighter.

"Say your prayers, bitch."

Oh my God, he thinks that's original? I take a step, he makes a minute movement. In a split-second, my ears are ringing, he stumbles backwards and drops the rifle on the floor. I raise a shaking hand to my face, startled when I feel the sticky wetness. I look down at myself, my stomach churning.

"Are you all right?" Robyn asks, her tone tight and intense. I nod, my gaze going from her holstering the gun to the man who's now still. I move to reach for the mask.

"No, don't touch him," she says sharply. She reaches for a pair of latex gloves, puts them on, and moves the mask aside. "You know this guy?"

I shake my head. "No, I've never seen him. One of Tony's hired goons, I assume."

"We'll figure it out." She goes for her phone next.

"What are you doing?"

"What do you think I'm doing? I have to call it in. You can notify your lawyer from the office, but this takes precedence."

Something is starting to unravel, and it's happening at the worst possible moment. What if he had pulled the trigger? Who was he here for in the first place—me? Her? A shitty job I did trying to protect her. She saved my life.

"I can't come with you."

"You'll have to."

"No...no." I walk backwards, holding up my hands. "This is not working. Either you come with me, or you have to let me go. There are people I need to speak to, especially now."

"Kendall. I have to call it in." Her tone is calm, patient, and at this moment, it doesn't do a damn thing for me. I draw my own weapon a split-second before she goes for hers. I'm sure she's not planning on using it on me, just as I'm not going to do anything stupid. It gives me the element of surprise, and I flee from the scene. I know she won't follow me, because she must deal with the dead body on the hallway floor.

I run all the way to my car and start the engine. Family dinner and uncomfortable conversations will have to be moved up. Most of all I have to assure everyone that there's still a way in which we won't lose everything, and the ones responsible for my father's death will be held accountable.

Chapter Twenty-Three

What the hell did you do? I could ask Kendall the question if she was still here. I could ask myself the same question because I should have known this could never work out. Just because she'd been tending to me for a couple of days, because we've had an intimate, blazing hot connection—that doesn't mean Kendall is ready to give up on any of the privileges that running the Mancini clan gives her.

I know that finding her father's killer is her priority, and I won't give up trying.

This is bad.

I can't even begin to process the dead hitman. I know I had to shoot him. He was ready to pull the trigger, and I couldn't have that happen. We need her as a witness. I'm not kidding myself into thinking that doing my job was my only incentive. Either way, no one is going to blame me, but I have to go through the right channels.

What Kendall considers to be the right channels is very different from the lawful approach. Pride in family tradition. What an awful mess. We're of an age where you can't blame your parents for everything that goes awry in your life, but there's no doubt that they've contributed to the two of us being in this situation.

Hampton arrives with a couple of other agents. I guess we can all drop the pretense now.

"Robyn, are you okay?" It still says *Jessica Byrne* on the door.

"He was coming after Kendall. I had to shoot him. She says he's not familiar, but he might be Bianco's. They hire out."

Hampton gives me a strange look I don't know how to interpret.

"We are close."

"What happened to you?" he asks, and it's only then that I remember he hasn't seen me since my run-in with Bruno. "Where is she now?"

"Too many questions at once." He's not the only one giving me strange looks which I probably deserve for making jokes while standing next to a dead man. "Okay. Bruno went rogue, and he thought he'd deliver me to her. You know, the way a cat shows off a rat to their owner thinking it's a great idea? She wasn't having it, told him off. Come to think of it, he could be behind this, though I'm not sure he has these kinds of contacts. They cut him off."

"Okay. Where is Ms. Mancini?"

I have to be very careful about what I say next.

"We'll continue as planned, at least I hope you ironed out something with the AUSA that we can present. I'll meet with him later, but obviously I couldn't just leave this guy here. We have to ID him ASAP."

"Robyn, hold on for a second." He steers me away to a corner of the hallway as the medical examiner's team begins their work. "We'll take care of it. There's something I need to show you as well, and we should bring her in right now."

"What? No, it's too early for that. We move too fast, and we'll end up with nothing. She's not going to give us anything if she thinks we'll play her."

"She might not have a choice," he says.

"This," I point to the dead man, "is not her fault. He was going to kill her."

"I don't doubt it, but that's a bit beside the point, isn't it? Her running away wasn't the deal. I believe what you gave us is more than enough to bring her in, and from there, it's her choice."

I know that this is generous. Kendall sits at the top of a crumbling pyramid, and the best she can do for herself is to help us clean up. I believe that a part of her wants to.

"What is it you wanted to show me?"

"In the car," he says. "Come with me."

A few minutes later I'm spellbound as he shows me the video. Someone at the infamous fundraiser is going around with a camera. Startled, I recognize my dad standing next to Alphonso Mancini.

"Why did Bianco tell Kendall that my father might have killed hers? If he came to this event as a friend of the Mancinis, he wasn't armed."

"It makes no sense, but Bianco being this obvious doesn't make sense either. He knows Kendall would come after him with everything she's got, and that's not in his interest either."

I continue to watch. There are more familiar faces, other members of the Mancini family.

"Where did you get this?"

"Marina Fiori kept it in a safe deposit box. Apparently, the list she gave Mancini was not complete."

What could be her reasoning, I wonder? Additional security? She wasn't sure who she could trust? And then my jaw drops.

"What is Bruno doing there?"

"Why are you surprised? He rarely left Alphonso's side."

"Yes, but he told Kendall he wasn't there."

We share a look.

"Speaking of things that don't make sense. He's a bit of a creep, but he hasn't really shown his true colors until recently. I don't think Kendall would tolerate that."

"Robyn, think about what you just said."

I do. It all makes sense.

"Wow. I'm not sure what exactly that means, but he has had an ongoing obsession with Kendall. She told him off not long ago, so if he sent someone after her right away, that's bad. He pretends that Alphonso wanted to see them married, but what if that's not true? If Alphonso told him he had no chance, would Bruno try to get him out of the way? Try to convince Kendall that her best option to keep family and business together would be to marry him?"

"It's a damn soap opera," he says with a sigh.

"She's under a lot of pressure. It might have worked."

"Don't tell me you feel sorry for the princess."

"I'm wondering if he was working alone. If he kept up the charade for this long, he can't have trusted that many people, even if some of the Mancinis openly or secretly agreed with him." Something springs to mind, and I sit up straight. "How sure are we that Angela Mancini died of natural causes?"

The way Hampton looks at me, I'm afraid he's going to say I need to take a break. To my relief, he answers, "Pretty sure. She was sick. But in order to answer those questions, we need to lean on Kendall. The AUSA is interested in making it a little less painful if she gives us names. And given that Bruno might have played a role in her father's death, she should be motivated."

"We'll meet with the AUSA first," I say. "We'll look into Mrs. Mancini's death, and Bruno, and I'll bring you Kendall. I promise. Give me twenty-four hours."

He hesitates for a few nail-biting moments, then he nods. "Okay, let's do it your way. For now."

Kendall, you better not let me down.

I've looked at Bruno before, obviously. The almost son-in-law. I'm poring over the same pictures as before, looking at them from a new perspective.

I also texted Kendall to let her know we need to talk. I need to know that she's okay. This part is tricky. The more we find out, the more other people might want to step forward and try to get their own deal. I'm not holding my breath that it could be Bruno, but in case he saw an opportunity to get back at her...I don't want to go there, not yet.

The meeting with the prosecutor isn't very uplifting either.

"This is highly unusual," he says. "You are giving her a lot of time to get rid of evidence."

"We have a lot of evidence already, and she knows that," Hampton, fortunately, backs me up.

"Above all, Kendall Mancini wants to know who killed her father," I add. "She understands what's at stake."

"You got made."

I'm fairly proud of myself for holding his gaze without blushing. The men in the room don't need to know everything.

"Bruno likely had a contact. We'll figure it out. I know everything about this is unusual, but it's an unusual case. Kendall trusts me. It will work in our advantage."

He raises an eyebrow, no doubt a commentary to my bruises.

"She and Bruno used to be close, but she drew a line after this," I reach up to touch the side of my face. "Their relationship is irreparable, especially if we can show her that he had a hand in Al Mancini's death. We get him for the embezzlement, assault, and the murder...She'll give us everything we need."

"What about Tony Bianco?"

"I want to bring him in for a friendly talk," I say. "There's a reason why he wanted to frame my father. It would make sense that he knows who really pulled the trigger."

I'm on a roll. It all fits together, right? Those men would rather bite off their tongues than talk, but if Kendall can help us get to them, she might be off the hook. That's a huge incentive.

"What can I tell her? If this works out, is it realistic to think about immunity?"

During those seconds of tense silence, I'm painfully aware that not only her future is on the line, and a happy ending for both of us is highly unlikely.

Tony Bianco is having lunch with two of his sons, and a business partner from the looks of it. Predictably, two men belonging to his security staff step in our way.

This is not completely unfamiliar, to him or us.

"I'm sorry, lady, but you can see I'm in the middle of something here. I don't have time to chat."

"Oh, I think you'll want to make time. The outcome could be quite interesting for you."

"You're trying to charm me into coming with you? That's new." He smiles.

"Or I could just get the AUSA on the line, but then this would go beyond a chat."

Tony looks me up and down, then he laughs.

"Agent Johnson, I appreciate a good bluff. What do you want to know?"

"Not here. We'll have to discuss some sensitive information. Believe me, you'll find this works better in a more private setting."

Bianco shrugs, the smile still on his face a stark contrast to his sons' angry expressions. "You heard the lady. I suppose she won't mind if I get my lawyer on the way."

"Suit yourself, Mr. Bianco," I say.

Still no news from Kendall. After this, I'll have to figure something out. Fast.

Bianco is comfortable. I want him to be, to think that this is not about him, or the way he tried to frame my father.

"Can I get you anything? A coffee?"

That greatly amuses him. "Please, Agent, don't insult me."

"Very well. Jimmy Bruno."

Bianco sobers up immediately, sits up straighter. "It's a damn shame. He had potential."

"So, you're aware of recent events?" I keep it vague on purpose.

"That the princess kept leading him on for decades or so and now kicked him out on his behind? Everyone's aware of that."

"You know Mr. Bruno well?"

Both Bianco and his lawyer frown. The latter shakes his head.

"You had my client come here to ask him that? I'm sorry, Agent, but that's a new low."

"Bear with me for a moment. This is about Mr. Bianco's expertise."

"Expertise?" He seems to enjoy this most of all. "Yes, you could say I have it. Jimmy and Alphonso were both fooling themselves. They gave her time, the business, she kept asking for more, but was never willing to give back to the family."

"You're talking about Kendall Mancini."

"Of course. Alphonso was an old-fashioned guy, like me, but he was also soft. So, he kept stalling Jimmy until, I guess, he had enough."

"That means what? Jimmy killed Mr. Mancini because he couldn't marry his daughter?"

"I didn't say that, but it's a theory, right? You must have thought of that."

"You have a lot of theories, Mr. Bianco."

"You can't bury your head in the sand when you have a business to run. It's important that I keep myself informed, know the playing field, but that can't come as a surprise to you."

"It doesn't. Why didn't you share that theory with Kendall? Why send her on a wild goose chase instead?"

He shrugs. "What do you think? I don't care about their drama. She's a competitor. If she's distracted, that's only good for us. And she came to me, asking questions."

"Maybe she just wants closure."

"Don't we all? As you can see, I couldn't help her with that, and I'm not sure how I can help you."

"Let's go back to Mr. Bruno for a moment. What other reason might he have for wanting Alphonso, and maybe even Kendall's mother, out of the way?"

"This has been nice, Agent, but I'm afraid I have a business to run. If you don't have anything else, I'd like to leave now."

"One more thing, Mr. Bianco. I'd like to tell you a theory of my own. For a while, we thought that Mr. Bruno was working alone, and that his main goal was to get to the Mancini empire—" He snorts at that expression, just like I expected. "Via Kendall. But then we realized something...He's not the only one benefiting from Alphonso's death, and in order to pull it off, he needed help."

"Sure. You might want to ask *your* father about that, Agent Johnson. I hear he's been around the Mancinis a lot."

"My father was trying to get Alphonso to turn himself in, and he almost succeeded. Alphonso's death changed the dynamics drastically, made it look like it was the FBI's fault, but also...like there might be a mole, and the Mancini clan could be in disarray."

"You're not making a lot of sense. I'd like to leave."

"Jimmy Bruno was never the mastermind, and he isn't now. He wanted the money and power that would have come with marrying Kendall, and of course he wanted her. He wasn't thinking big...like Arturo Rossi, for example. Or you."

"I don't like what you're implying. Let's keep it polite, shall we? I'm going to leave. Now."

"There were a lot of calls between you and Mr. Bruno on the day of Al Mancini's death."

"If that's all...?" The lawyer interjects.

"Yes, that's all for now," I say. "I imagine we'll continue our conversation soon. Have a nice day."

Bianco's demeanor is a lot less friendly when he and the lawyer leave the office in a hurry.

"Things are going to happen," Hampton comments.

"Oh yes, they will."

Chapter
Twenty-Four

I am frantic. When I reach my condo, I lock myself in and tell security staff not to let anyone in unless I tell them. I'm only able to stop for a moment and breathe after I've washed the blood off me and changed into a new shirt and suit. Hair, make-up, going through the familiar motions distracts me from the chaos I was surrounded by only an hour ago.

I can't have chaos. I know I have to move up the meeting, get my family in here and make sure we're on the same page when it comes to the next steps. Some of them might not like me very much, but they'll come together once they learn what happened.

I make a few calls, the last one to *Catania* to prepare and deliver lunch, and then I instruct security once again. Frantic.

I ignore Robyn's calls, because there's nothing much I can tell her until this is solved.

To my surprise, Uncle Lorenzo arrives first. He takes the wine, but we have barely made it to the dining room before he starts berating me. He's furious. Not because I almost got killed.

"God, your father would be so ashamed right now. Everything is falling apart because of you, and it's only been a few months since Angela passed away."

I already regret offering him a drink.

"What are you talking about? Nothing is falling apart, except maybe Jimmy. This has been a long time coming. We need to replace him, and I have some ideas."

"To be frank, Kendall, no one gives a damn about your ideas. Your father might have been able to look the other way, but we can't, not anymore. You're risking the family, everything my grandparents built, for what? Your 'alternative' lifestyle," he spits.

"That's enough. My parents trusted me with the business. Not you, not Luca. Jimmy Bruno sent someone after me today. I can't have that, and I can't have family members stabbing me in the back."

"You are so painfully naïve."

"That might be, but I hold the majority of the shares. You should remember that, Uncle Lorenzo."

"It's sick. You and Luca both, but at least he was smart enough not to flaunt it, have a real marriage. I don't blame Jimmy for finally having enough of your stupidity. You could have had a good life with him. You threw it away."

I shake my head. I knew things were bad the last time we talked, and when Luca revealed that he helped Jimmy abduct Robyn to make Lorenzo proud or something...but this is beyond the pale. It's the last thing I need from family right now.

"You forget one thing. I am not the enemy here, and neither is Luca. The FBI agent, I'll take care of that, but it's really Tony Bianco they're after. And that's good for us."

"Luca says they have evidence."

"Mild stuff. We might pay a fine, but that's not even clear yet. Tony and his clan are bigger fish, and they consider them more dangerous."

166

I want to shake some sense into him. I'm aware there's no time for it, and besides, it wouldn't work. I'll pick my battles.

"So, you're planning on becoming a rat?"

He's testing my patience, and my focus.

"You're going to call me a rat for giving them information on the Biancos? Wow, that's interesting. It makes me wonder whose side you are on."

He makes a dismissive gesture.

"Whatever. You say you can contain the situation?"

"Yes. But I'm afraid we need to do more about Jimmy."

"You shut him out. What more do you want to do?"

At least I don't have to answer right now, as my other guests arrive. One by one they file into the room. Luca and Elena arrive with their mother. Claudia and Marc have brought their kids. I think of small sticky fingerprints on floor-to-ceiling windows, testimony of how tired I am. It's nothing in the big scheme of things. Nothing that can't be undone. Sofia is the last to arrive, as usual quiet and polite, as if she was trying to make herself invisible.

"Thank you all for coming," I say when everyone is seated around the table. "I think we're all aware that there isn't a lot of time to do this, so here it goes. Jessica's name is Robyn Johnson, and she works with the FBI. She's going to help us find out who killed my father."

I'm not surprised that most of my guests talk at the same time, trying to raise their voices over one another.

"Please, listen to me for a moment." I could have done without Lorenzo rolling his eyes. Everyone else sits in tense silence. "I know this is...unusual. We've been through some difficult times, but I'm sure we can make this work to our advantage. Most of all, I'll finally be able to keep the promise I made to my mother in her last moments. You know she asked this one thing of me. Robyn—Agent Johnson—also wants to find out what happened that night."

"What does she want in return?" Claudia asks.

"She already knows that Jimmy stole from the company. He'll have to answer for that, for kidnapping and beating her."

I see Luca pale at that, and I can't say I'm sorry.

"Jimmy made a number of big, irreversible mistakes over time, and frankly, he made his bed. But the FBI wants to go after Bianco, and there's our advantage. Whatever you can help with, I appreciate it."

Marc looks doubtful. "Did she give you any reassurances?" he asks. "How do we know she's not lying, and they'll come for us one by one?"

"The accounts are safe. They are a lot more interested in the murders, and the drug trade on the Bianco side, and apparently, they are still trying to figure out what happened with the raid. This is in their interest, and ours."

"Sounds nice, doesn't it?" Lorenzo mutters. "Everyone's happy. Except it will never work like that. I say if Kendall wants to go on a suicide mission, let her, but I won't be along for the ride."

I can see the doubt in their faces.

"Lorenzo is wrong. But I'll take responsibility for what happened on my watch. I want my father's murderer to be held accountable, and if Tony Bianco had a hand in it, I want him to go down, hard. I know that you all cared about my parents. This is our best bet."

I'm aware of Sofia wringing her hands in her lap, and I'm sorry. This has got to bring up bad memories for her.

"I don't think so," Lorenzo argues. "You had your chance, and you blew it. You think Jimmy is a danger, or Bianco is, you should take a break. Go somewhere with a non-extradition treaty, let us do the work."

To my surprise—and probably, his—Anna speaks up. "We would all like to know why Alphonso died."

"Sure, and sometimes it's better to let sleeping dogs lie. Nothing is going to bring him back, or Angela. We can only avoid making the same mistakes they made when they thought a woman could run the business."

"Oh come on, Dad, are you even listening to yourself?" Claudia finishes her glass in one swallow, a quick, frustrated gesture. "You sound like someone from a different century."

"Watch your mouth! There are children around here."

"What if I don't? Kendall's not stupid. She says the accounts are safe, I don't think she's lying to us. Uncle Alphonso had friends in law enforcement. It kept them off our backs, and that is never a bad thing. You're just mad at Luca for no reason and taking it out on everyone."

I didn't see that one coming—or Uncle Lorenzo jumping to his feet and storming out of the room.

"Okay," I say after we've heard the door slam. "Anyone has any other questions?"

"That FBI agent, do you really trust her?" Claudia asks.

I don't have to think about it. "I know she wants to do what's best for the safety of everyone in this city. Dismantling our business is not the way to do it, and she knows it. Besides, she likes the food at *Catania* too much." That might have been a stretch, but to my relief, I see a few smiles.

Sofia Bianco isn't smiling. "It wouldn't surprise me if Tony is behind all this," she says. "If you have the chance to bring him down, I beg you, do it."

Her quiet determined tone sends a shiver down my spine. Uncle Lorenzo's bigotry be damned, we are doing the right thing.

We still have to find an adequate solution regarding Jimmy. The authorities will deal with him sooner or later. I'm not sure that will be enough.

Chapter
Twenty-Five

Dealing with Bianco has substantially cut into my twenty-four hours, but I'm finally standing in the lobby of the building that houses Kendall's condo. I have news to bring. More than expected.

Some very bad news too. There's no turning back. If I can't convince her today, all bets are off.

A burly security guard stops me from entering the elevator.

"Please check with Ms. Mancini," I say. "She's expecting me."

He makes a quick call and, with a shrug, steps aside. So far so good.

I haven't even started to process my relationship with Kendall, and how it might help or hinder in the future. Perhaps no one ever has to know. I don't have time to feel melancholic about it either. No time to feel anything.

The security guard upstairs got the memo. With an impassive expression, she leads me to the front door and announces my arrival.

I know right away I'm walking into something important, an impromptu family gathering. She said she'd check with me first.

Kendall, glass of wine in hand, gets up to greet me as if I hadn't tried to get to her all day.

"Robyn, welcome. As you can imagine, we were just talking about you. I assume we should take this to my office?"

When I notice the expectant gazes on me, I change gears. "This is something you all need to know. We are looking for Jimmy Bruno. If he contacts any of you, please let the authorities know. It's important."

Kendall has dropped the smile. "Like I said, let's go to my office." She takes my arm and all but physically drags me from the room. I realize that I wanted to stall. Everything.

When we are inside her office and the door is closed, she says, "I know you were trying to reach me. I'm sorry for this morning, but I had to talk to everyone first."

"About what?"

"About the fact that you're not the enemy which is to your advantage now. I can promise you there's no one in this room who'd feel sorry for Bianco and his clan. Or Jimmy, actually. Uncle Lorenzo still likes him, but he stormed out a few hours ago."

"Kendall."

"You didn't come here to arrest me, did you? That guy was trying to kill me. You shot him, for which I'm grateful, but...what's going on?"

I feel beyond exhausted.

"I have to tell you something. Your Uncle Lorenzo was found dead."

Her hand goes to her mouth.

"We don't know yet who did it, but it's even more important now that you work with us."

She seems to only now remember that she's still holding the glass, and she sets it down on the shiny surface of the desk.

"If I remember correctly, you promised me something."

"Yes. We were able to put some of the pieces together regarding your father's death. It's not one hundred percent clear yet, but it looks like Jimmy Bruno teamed up with Bianco."

"He promised him one of his daughters?" Kendall asks bitterly. "Damn it. This is bad. I wanted Lorenzo held accountable for his bullshit, not dead. What are you doing about Bianco?"

"Watch him for now, but he keeps incriminating himself. Seems like he did make a lot of promises to Bruno."

"Jimmy was running out of patience."

I nod. "He realized that you were never going to marry him, and your parents wouldn't force you. That meant his access to the business would always be limited. But if he got in bed with the Biancos, it meant he could eventually get back at your parents, and you."

"Wow. That's...elaborate."

"It sure is. I'm sorry." Because it's not yet the end of the bad news. "You got everything in order with your family?"

"I did," she says with a sigh. "That is, until you told me about Lorenzo. Luca and Claudia are in there. I have to tell them."

"I can—"

"No," she interrupts me brusquely. "There will be consequences, and everyone needs to step up. How did he die?"

"He was shot in the back," I say, seeing her wince. "Kendall, you know that I'll need you to come with me, right?"

"You'll need to wait until they're gone."

"I can't promise you that."

She holds my gaze, maybe trying to stare me down, but I can't make any more compromises, much as I wish.

"I upheld my part of the bargain. From the conversations we are tracking, and from what we could recover, it was Jimmy who pulled the trigger, with Tony's blessing." I take a deep breath, if only to prolong the inevitable. "I shouldn't tell you this, but we're also looking into your mother's death."

"What? She was sick. This is not helping anyone."

"Jimmy Bruno and Tony Bianco thought that when they got your father out of the way, the business would crumble. Your mother stepped in, and you were more successful than before. She got sick, but it might not have been fast enough for either of them."

For the first time, I can tell there are cracks in her composure. I wish we could end the day in a different way, but it's much too late for that, too many crimes, too many people hurt and killed.

"We'll get them both," I promise. "But first, I need you to come with me."

She nods. "Give me ten minutes. Can I call my lawyer from there? You're not arresting me, are you?"

"No. We just have to make it official that you're helping us get to Bianco."

"I'm sorry you got hurt."

"It wasn't your fault."

"No, it wasn't," she says, pensive. "All right, let's do this."

I stay in a corner at a respectful distance while Kendall delivers the bad news. The chaos has begun even though it didn't start with the story and the players we expected. Lorenzo Mancini was a man of many prejudices, not exactly a good guy, but this is still a grieving family.

I think of the prosecutor's words. Lorenzo's wife and kids might have to make some business decisions, but it's Kendall who knows the skeletons in everyone's closet.

We have the evidence we need. Jessica Byrne delivered a treasure trove.

After everyone has left, Kendall picks up her purse and keys. She reconsiders and turns back to her office. From the doorway, I watch as she unlocks a cabinet and takes out a couple of files.

"This will be interesting for you," she says. "I hope after that, you'll leave me and my family alone."

Saying sorry again wouldn't make a difference, I know, but I'm tempted.

Kendall isn't done though. When we sit in the car, she takes my hand, holding it for several seconds. I should pull away, but I don't.

"Thank you," she says. "This took more detours than expected, but I guess this is it."

I still have no words.

~ell~

Nothing is ever this easy. I had hoped that Lorenzo Mancini being murdered minutes after leaving Kendall's condo, and Bruno still on the run, would be the only complications of the day. They're not.

We're only a few blocks away from the office when I realize we're being followed. The driver of the black van isn't even sneaky about it. We're in the middle of the city, and he keeps creeping closer and closer.

"We're almost there." Who am I trying to reassure?

"Well, you told me not to bring my gun, so I hope no one else is going to get killed today," Kendall says dryly. "Perhaps it's time to duck."

However, the driver seems to have other plans. In the middle of the road, he slams into my rear bumper, both of us lurching forward. Who knows that we are on our way? An uncomfortable thought forms on my mind. With Bianco being under surveillance, and Bruno on the run...There aren't a lot of people who know or could guess where we are going.

The driver moves in again.

"Almost there, right?"

I call for backup, struggling to keep my voice calm as the vehicle makes contact again.

Kendall reaches for her purse and takes out a small handgun.

"What the hell—?"

"Be glad I don't always listen to you." She aims it at the other car's tires. At the same moment, we hear sirens, and the driver takes a sharp turn, wheels on the sidewalk as backup moves in. Around us, other cars have already moved out of the way, and I finally come to a halt.

Backup is here, but things aren't going exactly as planned when they yell at Kendall to drop the gun.

She does and raises her hands while giving me a wry smile.

"Well. You're up. I trust you to do this the right way, Agent Johnson."

Chapter Twenty-Six

"**P**lease, go with them. I'll be right there."

Half an hour later, there's still no sight of Robyn. I assume she is making some inquiries regarding the driver, but I'm starting to get worried. I took all the precautions I possibly could, and I think the business is protected. Still, that phone call to my lawyers is looking more and more urgent.

My assets are protected. What if I am not?

No.

What I told the family earlier is still true. Lorenzo was wrong to assume I let it all slip away easily. Robyn and I agree on some things. The city will be safer without men like Bianco and Bruno trying to get their piece of the pie. That was the deal. I'm still in control.

After twenty more minutes, the door opens, and I get to my feet. It's not Robyn, but her colleague Hampton McKay. I remember him talking to her at the scene.

"I assume I can have my phone call now. Where is Agent Johnson?"

"She's a little busy right now, but she'll be with you soon. Why don't we get started meanwhile?"

"I'd feel better if my lawyer was present for that conversation."

"Are you worried about anything, Ms. Mancini? We know you have a license for that gun in your purse."

"Good. Do I need to worry about anything else? Robyn said you wanted to talk about the Biancos, and Jimmy Bruno. It seems like you have more than enough evidence against them, after everything that happened. Just in case..." I push the folders I brought with me, towards him. "I keep a lot of notes. Of things I hear, what people tell me. So did my father. I can't vouch for the accuracy of everything, but I guess you have your resources."

"We appreciate that. Would you like a coffee? We might be here for a while."

"Please don't take this the wrong way, but you know I own several restaurants. So, no, thank you, I don't think I'd like your coffee."

"That's such a cliché but suit yourself. Tell me about what I'm going to find in that folder."

"Not much on Jimmy, I'm afraid, but I can tell you about my experiences with him. Of course, I had no idea how far he was going to go."

"No? You couldn't tell that he'd do whatever he thought made you happy?"

There's something about his tone that I don't like.

"Anyway, Tony not only being the jerk that he is, but also a competitor, I had to do my research on him. I trust that Robyn told me the truth and it won't come back to bite me, especially after everything you found out about him."

"I'm really sorry about your parents and your uncle," McKay says. He sounds sincere enough, so I humor him.

"Thank you." It seems a tad out of the blue, still. "We assume that it's all part of the Bruno-Bianco conspiracy?"

"Robyn is working on that. Speaking of which, can you tell me when exactly you learned that Bruno had abducted her, and who else was involved?"

We're wading into dangerous territory. As much as I despise Luca's actions, I've known Lorenzo all my life, and for that I gave him a second chance. Also, for Elena. Jimmy and Tony are the bad guys here. Let's not confuse that.

"I know what you want to say, but I had to make sure she was okay first. We didn't come back from the cabin until this morning. I took care of a few things from afar, blocking his access to business accounts and such."

"So, you did get a lot done, but it didn't occur to you to report him?"

"Why would I? I assumed Robyn would take care of that, and frankly, I had other things on my mind."

"Getting in touch with your lawyers and hiding your offshore accounts?"

"I hope you're fishing, Agent McKay. I really hope that because this is not the deal Robyn and I made." I make a dismissive gesture when he opens his mouth. "I'm aware that she's not authorized to make a deal in the true sense of the word. Stop putting words in my mouth. I handled Bruno. I was under the impression you'd take care of him when you found out that he was responsible for murdering my father. Frankly, before Robyn told me—I just wanted him gone, and Robyn didn't say otherwise. No, I was busy keeping it together after getting shot at, and then telling my family that my uncle had been murdered as well." I stop to take a breath. McKay is waiting. "We talk about Bianco, or I'm leaving. You have nothing to hold me here."

"I wouldn't count on that. You fired a gun in the middle of traffic."

"To protect myself and one of your agents."

He leans back in his chair, crossing his arms over his chest.

"You're bluffing," I accuse.

"I'm afraid I'm not. Of course, you can call your lawyer, that's up to you. Or you can lay it all on the table and help us put the Biancos away for good. I know you're tired. Why don't you give yourself a break?"

"I want to speak to Robyn."

"First, let me lay out what's in it for you. The AUSA is willing to be lenient if we can do this quick and easy."

"Really?" This can't be happening. I knew that I'd have to spend some time, go along with the game, and give them something too, but not this. "That means immunity?"

"That means you'll finally have closure. You've been at this for a long time. You know that we can't look the other way on everything."

"I didn't murder anyone or sell drugs to kids. I want my lawyer now."

"Okay. Come with me."

When I get up, for a brief moment, it feels like the floor gives beneath my feet. I don't know what to believe anymore...I'm in more trouble than I expected. It's not over yet.

Chapter
Twenty-Seven

I curse when the hot coffee burns my tongue. I wish I could be back in my apartment, Jessica Byrne, small business owner. Then, maybe I could turn a blind eye to the dealings of my lover, dine at *Catania*, pretend that whatever goes on behind that door, on the other side of the counter, is none of my business.

Instead, I watch on a monitor as she and her lawyer confer with the AUSA.

I can see the disbelief on her face when she realizes that the prosecutor is not going to completely ignore her involvement in illegal transactions. Even I was a bit blindsided, and that says a lot. I'd grown close. Too close. No one's saying it yet, but they might soon.

I'm not sure if Kendall is going to keep silent. I had to betray her all over again. Better to have her here than waiting for Jimmy or Bianco to strike again. Everything is better than that, even knowing that she probably hates me right now.

"The stuff in those folders, it's good, right?"

Hampton, who has stepped outside, nods. "Pretty good. Turns out this was some sort of opposition research that Al Mancini had done. With the help of Blake, no less."

"It's no wonder that Bianco wanted Kendall to blame him. She seems ready. Is she still going to do time?"

He looks at me in surprise. "Robyn, did you even look at what we were able to find?"

"Sure. Bruno stole from her. He was involved in some tax evasion schemes that she might or might not have known about, but the AUSA said we could work something out."

"Why does this matter so much to you?"

I shrug, uncomfortable under his scrutiny. "I don't know. I've done undercover assignments before. It seems that save for her parents, she was surrounded by misogynistic and homophobic assholes."

"For that she has my sympathy. It's not an excuse to evade taxes and launder money. Like Bianco, she had goons she sent after people that didn't act the way she wanted. You know that, Robyn."

"I do." I suppress a sigh. "While she's waiting for the lawyer, you think I could have a word?"

"We talked about this. Boss prefers if you didn't. Let her think it over."

"Yeah."

"You don't sound too happy about it. Be proud. It's finally time to topple all of them."

He's right, I'm not happy, but he can't know the reason. I'm not just nervous because Kendall might tell on me, or what it could do to my career. I know she's not innocent. For the first time in my life, doing the right thing feels utterly wrong.

It's late when I'm finally able to leave the office, feeling defeated and tired. I still call my parents and see if they're up for seeing me.

"Have you eaten?" is the first thing my mother asks, and I nearly cry. It's not because of one thing, it's the sum of them. I didn't manage to speak to Kendall—I hope I can redeem that tomorrow. Now that the day is coming to a close, all I can think of is the gunman waiting for us this morning. Bruno breaking down the door to my apartment.

Damn them all.

"You mean you have some leftovers?"

"Sweetie, of course."

She might have heard something in my voice. But she's lived with my father for a long time, so she's aware of the stakes, and generally observant.

At this moment, I'm just so grateful they're still here, unlike Al and Angela Mancini.

I wish Bruno was behind bars. Once we have him, the dominoes will start to fall. Until that is the case, we can't really rest, but I still have to eat.

"That's awesome. Thank you so much. I'll be there in a few."

"I have a chocolate cream pie too. If I can convince your father to leave you some..."

I laugh, and then stop, realizing how close I am to crying.

Hampton is right. I stopped a murderer, and the driver of the car hitting us on purpose is in custody as well. The evidence against Bianco is mounting.

It's a good outcome. I have to tell myself that, but as I'm driving out to my parents' home, my mind wanders back to the cabin, and Kendall taking care of me. She might have done some shady things, but she's not all bad either. I've seen another side, and I refuse to believe that it was all a ruse—like Jessica Byrne.

For a moment, I think that the dark blue Sedan is following me, but I realize the day is catching up with me when the driver turns. I continue the road all the way to my parents' house and park on the curb.

Inside, they greet me like it's a normal time for a family dinner.

We sit down to eat, and Dad fills our glasses with red wine.

"If you like a bit more, you could always call a cab," he says. "Or stay overnight."

"Thank you, but I look forward to sleeping in my own bed. It's been busy."

"So we've heard." He and Mom exchange a look I'm not sure how to interpret. They probably caught the news today. Even if my name wasn't mentioned, the story of Lorenzo Mancini's death was picked up by the news outlets. A shooting, a pursuit...they might not know for sure, but suspect something. At least I was able to hide the bruises Bruno gave me, under make-up. Mostly. "Are you okay?"

"I am. I just wanted to see you both...and a hot meal doesn't hurt," I joke. "Big case...I've had a lot of take-out and frozen."

"Kendall Mancini was arrested."

Please, God, no. I wish I could escape the subject for a few hours, but then I think about the fact that I'm having a dinner with my parents while she's in a holding cell—alone. Never mind the danger her ways of doing business exposed us both to, and that prior to this day, she's lived in extreme luxury. I can't bring myself to condemn her for that.

I don't know how to feel about her, because the first, instinctive approach was obviously wrong. I fell for her.

"Dad, you know I can't talk about a case."

"We're aware you can't tell us details, of course," Mom says. "But do you think I wasn't aware Dad was friends with Alphonso?"

My jaw must have dropped. She laughs. "Well, that's marriage. We share everything."

"I'm not sure I want to know."

"You never met him, did you?" Dad asks. "He was charming, could talk people into most everything. From what I learned, Kendall is pretty much the same."

I can't disagree so far.

"Don't tell this to anyone, but we are pretty close to finding out what exactly happened that night."

"With Bruno being on the run, I can imagine. I had warned Al about him, but he didn't want to hear any of it. Jimmy was like a son to him, even though he knew Kendall wasn't interested. He still would have liked to see them together."

"But that would have never happened. Jimmy saw the writing on the wall, and he went to look for other coalitions." I need to stop drinking. Mom is looking far too interested, and I shouldn't be talking about any of this.

I screwed up.

"I had no proof at the time. It's good that the truth is finally coming out," Dad says, pensive.

"I agree."

He holds out the bottle, and I shake my head, then reconsider. "Okay, why not. I'll take a cab and fall straight into bed."

"That sounds like a good plan. You can leave your keys and I'll drive your car over tomorrow morning." He gets up. "I'll make some coffee. I assume Mom told you about the chocolate cream pie?"

"She did. I wouldn't miss that for anything."

There are not enough comforts in the world to make things right, but I'll take the ones I can have now.

After another glass, coffee, and pie, I say goodbye to Mom and Dad, thinking that I might have to come back for a conversation about the Mancinis. There's still something strange about his abrupt departure, and I'm willing to bet I don't know the whole truth yet.

The cab company is supposed to send me someone within fifteen minutes of the call, but half an hour later I'm still standing on the curb shivering. I still plan to sleep in my own bed though, so I walk down the street, check my phone again...They should be here any moment. I'm almost on the corner when I see the Sedan again. Justified alarm or paranoia? I'll go with the former. I pretty much know my parents' neighbors, and neither one of them has a car like this. Unless they changed recently?

I take a closer look, wishing that damn cab would arrive. Nothing out of the ordinary. Maybe I am paranoid, that, or I need a good night's sleep. Ironic that I had some of my best sleep next to a criminal who might be indicted soon. I still think it's...unfair? No matter how much money she has, or spent, some of which wasn't hers, she still had to deal with all that crap.

People telling her that she wasn't enough, because she's a woman, and a lesbian. Like Kendall, I was lucky to have decent people for parents, but outside the safe sphere of the core family, I have dealt with some of the same things. I can relate. I feel the same incredulous anger.

We're still on different sides of the law.

I raise my hands, then stand still. Something in the air changed. Paranoia? Not so much. I take an educated guess.

"Jimmy? Whatever it is you're trying to do, don't be stupid. Kendall is in custody, and she doesn't give a damn about you. She's talking. We have you and Bianco on conspiracy. Don't make it worse."

"Jimmy? I don't know where he is, but I promise you that he'll pay for the role he played in this mess."

I slowly turn around, coming face to face with Tony Bianco.

"There I thought he was your golden boy."

"Get in the car. Please." I see that he's unarmed, but the two men arriving left and right, are not.

"The same goes for you. Didn't you hear what I said? We got you on conspiracy. You can be helpful, or you can make it worse."

"Do you have any idea how many cops and prosecutors have said this to me before? I tell you how this works. You'll come with me now. Otherwise, I might remember that your parents are living just up the street."

"We can talk about this."

Getting to this man, via the Mancinis, wasn't a bad idea. We just didn't move fast enough, I realize when I feel the distinct pressure of a gun against my back.

"Yes, let's talk somewhere else. Meanwhile, Princess will shut her mouth when she learns we have her girlfriend. Everyone wins."

That's not true though. Kendall will likely go away for a long time if she doesn't cooperate. She'll lose everything, the business, her freedom—and me because I'll possibly end up dead.

We're not there yet.

Chapter
Twenty-Eight

I t takes some time for the reality of my situation to sink in. My lawyer assured me that bail wouldn't be a problem, and the team would still work with the AUSA on the finer details. Until then, I'll have to keep my mouth shut, but they also warned me—holding back could cost me. Instead of being the material witness I'm spending the night in a holding cell like a common criminal, waiting to enter my plea.

Guilty.

Not guilty.

Does it even matter anymore?

They still need more evidence to bust Tony, and perhaps his sons, but what Robyn gave them on me was enough to keep me. The irony. Robyn. And Tony's master plan, using Jimmy's ego to destroy my family. I suppose he succeeded. I have no friends. People around me either want me dead or behind bars.

I'm still alive, I guess that counts for something.

I have no one. The realization is like a physical blow. Until this moment, I had no time to deal with the reality of it. I might have fooled myself into thinking I could hold business and family together, that

I might forge alliances with the women, modernize the organization...It's all gone.

For a long time, I was in denial about Jimmy, thinking that one day he could get over himself and be satisfied with being a business partner...Instead he worked with the enemy all along. My father often said there were no enemies, only those who had outsmarted us, but he, too, fell for a fantasy. Peaceful business deals, the idea that we could someday smooth over things with the Biancos, even after the Rossi affair.

What would he say now, knowing that Jimmy betrayed him, possibly had a hand in my mother's death?

Those are no longer theoretical musings, I realize, as the tears stream down my face. They surprise and embarrass me. I don't know when I even had time to cry last. In these walls, I'm forced to confront my demons as time is coming to a halt.

Everyone I loved has abandoned me. It wasn't a choice for my parents, but it definitely was for Robyn. She's on to the next case, probably has been told to stay away because she got a little too close to the target.

I am so tired.

I can't have slept more than a few minutes at a time, feeling jittery and exhausted at the same time when I hear the footsteps approach. I assume someone brings me breakfast. I have no appetite, and besides, I don't think the food in here will be anywhere near my standards. I'll make do until the bail hearing in the afternoon, and after that I'll hopefully be back home. Whatever that means.

I remember other members of my family taken in for an interview. None of them were ever convicted. I'll be fine.

My optimistic assessment is out the window when the man in uniform unlocks the cell and throws something—not breakfast—inside. He locks and walks away whistling. I take a closer look and then scream like I've wanted to for a long time.

I know what the dead rat means, before anyone bothers to give me explanations. I pray that I'm wrong, though I don't have high hopes.

There's frantic activity in and around my cell, people on phones. I hear someone calling for an ambulance. The poor person on staff who was actually tasked with delivering my breakfast might not make it. It's also a taste of what life in prison would look like for someone like me, though I might be safer there—if they thought I didn't talk.

They.

Tony. He has a lot of nerve, knowing that the FBI is watching him.

Someone finally removes the rat, and giving it one last look, I can't help myself and throw up.

I know what it means.

Robyn.

"Have you checked on Agent Johnson? Is she okay?"

The female guard doesn't answer my question, though she looks suspiciously sympathetic. "Let's get you cleaned up and get you breakfast."

"Really? You need to check on her. This was a message."

She doesn't comment but walks me to the bathroom in silence. I look at my face in the mirror, barely recognizing myself. Is that what a reckoning looks like? The bad guys win? I need to know what they did to her.

She must be alive, otherwise they wouldn't bother with a warning.

But I already gave the folder to the FBI, set things in motion that I can't take back.

I never imagined it was that obvious how much I cared for her. I don't have another breakdown, but I still refuse breakfast.

When McKay comes to see me, he looks like he's aged years since the last time.

"Will you tell me what happened to her? Like I already said a million times, I didn't know the man. He wore a guard's uniform, had a key. I thought he was bringing me breakfast—" My stomach lurches again, but there's nothing left to throw up. "Instead, he tossed a dead rat into the cell." I'm in another room now, guarded by even more personnel. It's hard to tell who they want to keep in, and out. I'm still sick to my stomach, and time is ticking. "It's Tony, right? He has Robyn?"

"Why are you so sure about that?" he asks.

"Because I know him."

"I'd assume that he's not the only one worried about secrets coming out."

"You're talking about...my family? No. None of them would ever do that to me. They knew that I—" I break off the sentence before I can blurt out something that I can't take back. Funny how a few hours ago I was ready to get back at her, reveal all about the tactics she used to get to me. But what if it wasn't all tactics? What if he's right? No. Never. Everyone might be talking behind everyone else's back—so they're prone to gossip, but they'd still stick with me.

"That you what?"

"Contrary to what you might think, I don't hate her, not even after I found out. She promised me to help find who killed my father, and she did. This was in the best interest of all my family, and they were aware of that. It was always about bringing down Tony, and, sadly, Jimmy. Have you found him yet?"

"We're still looking. Are you aware of any place where Tony might hold Agent Johnson?"

"Why would I be?"

"The information in those folders was fairly detailed. A good bargaining chip. If there's more, now is the time to share."

"I don't know anything. I swear."

"All right." He gets to his feet and turns to leave.

"Agent McKay? Will you let me know when you find her?"

I thought he was going to leave without an answer, but he turns to me one more time, looking as terrible as I feel.

"I'm sure you will find out, Ms. Mancini."

The door closes, the sound horribly final.

———

I'm about to go out of my skin when the door opens again, and my lawyer MacKenzie Winter walks in, looking serious. I all but jump to my feet.

"Do you have news on Agent Johnson? Can you tell me what happened?"

"We'll have to talk about your bail hearing," she says. "I need you to listen to me carefully, okay, Kendall? But first, there's someone here who wants to talk to you. Remember you don't have to." She goes back to the door, opens it, and to my surprise, Blake Ford walks in. Johnson. He, too, looks like he hasn't slept though his appearance is immaculate otherwise. Crisp shirt, suit, not a hair out of place. Not enough to mask the fear.

"Hello, Kendall," he says. "I was hoping we could have a word."

I shrug. "Sure. I'm not going anywhere." A guard stays in a corner, but my lawyer leaves to wait outside.

"You don't have to worry," he says as he sits down. "This isn't official business. You know that I'm retired."

"So I've heard. We can cut this short. I don't know where Robyn is. I wish I did, but I have no idea."

"I believe you." After a small, awkward pause, he continues. "Robyn came to see me and my wife late last night. You know that she cares about you."

This is taking a strange turn.

"I hope she's okay. That's what you wanted to tell me?"

"I knew your father very well. We were childhood friends, lost touch...Then later on—"

"You infiltrated my family and made him believe you were still his friend."

He doesn't deny the charge, at least not completely.

"Bianco had your father killed, and he needs to go down for that."

"Oh, I agree, but you might have heard about the package I received this morning. That complicates things."

"I can't tell you what to do, but I can tell you this. Al always told me that you were brave. He and Angela wanted the best future for you, and they wanted to clean up the business."

"I thought this wasn't official. They sent you in here to get a confession out of me without my lawyer present? Wow."

"There's been a lot of secrecy surrounding the night Al died. I think you deserve the whole truth."

"Jimmy was jealous and petty, and Tony offered to make all his dreams come true, isn't that what happened?"

"Yes, but there's more to it. They chose the fundraiser for a specific reason. I think Alphonso told Jimmy, and so Tony and Bruno moved up their plan. Al wanted to come in after that event."

I don't understand a thing.

"Come in..."

"As in come clean. Become an informant. He'd been having arguments with your uncle Lorenzo for a long time. He and Angela weren't happy about how Lorenzo was treating you, and his own son. He and I were preparing the next steps. Like I said, I can't tell you what to do with this, but you should know."

I sit, speechless.

"I know it's a lot to process. There might be others he told, though I doubt it. Jimmy was usually the first he went to after Angela. I'll come back if you want, but I need to speak to the agent now. Good luck, Kendall."

"Thank you," I say, still struck by those revelations, and what they mean. He leaves me with more questions than answers. When my mother practically asked me to declare a vendetta, was she serious, or was that the pain talking?

And Jimmy, damn him for betraying my family in multiple ways. He's going to find himself on the wrong end of an argument with Tony one day, no doubt about it.

MacKenzie comes back in, softly closing the door behind her.

"Let's start with the bad," she says, looking apologetic. It doesn't end. "You might have to surrender your passport. Worst case scenario, they'll insist on house arrest until the trial."

"I'll still have to pay bail, and for the house arrest?"

"They'll argue flight risk. At least you'd be home."

And no dead rats.

"That's the best you can do?"

"We're still negotiating," she says. "That's the good part."

There's not much left in terms of a silver lining...but I'm sure I can be a lot more helpful once I'm out of here. Make no mistake, I will be soon.

Chapter Twenty-Nine

A side from that one blow and some manhandling, they didn't get physical—so far. At this point, I'm still worth something to Bianco, and as long as that is the case, he'll keep me alive.

The situation can change at any moment.

In the car, they put a blindfold on me that hasn't come off yet. I was given some water earlier.

That's it.

My wrists are tied behind my back, much too tightly to bring them to the front and take off the blindfold. I'm indoors somewhere in the country, I assume. I heard the sound of birds when the sun came up. Beneath me, there's some sort of mattress. I'm close to the floor.

Tony Bianco's stupid ego trip. What does he think this is going to achieve? I'm mad at myself because I didn't see this coming. He took me for the same reason he had Alphonso Mancini killed, to keep the status quo, secrets under lock and key, but it's too late for that.

The question is what he'll do once he realizes that it's game over.

I'm angry because I have so many regrets, so many things left undone. I never managed to talk to Kendall, and now I might never have the chance. I hope she sees through his bullshit—whatever he wants to prevent from coming out, whatever happens, he'll likely kill me anyway.

She could still save herself. I hope she will.

I wish I could see her one more time.

I wish someone would come so I can finally pee.

My heart jumps into my throat when I hear the key in the lock, and I sit up, tense, in fight/flight mode. The trouble is I can't do either, so what's the next best thing? Play dead?

Within moments, there's a gun to my head, and a voice hisses, "Don't try anything."

I almost laugh, it's so absurd. The zip ties are cut, and someone ties my hands in front of me. Then the blindfold is ripped off and I'm hauled to my feet. I recognize the two men Bianco brought the other day. Keeping the gun trained on me, one of them directs me to the door. I'm getting a quick glimpse of the room, a spacious but sparsely furnished basement, before I'm pushed through the doorway and up a flight of stairs. The main floor is light and airy, big windows allowing a pretty view of the mountains and lake in the distance. I feel mocked.

They bring me to a huge den from which the view is even more amazing. The table is set for two, an amazing breakfast spread that makes my stomach growl, regardless of how inappropriate that reaction is.

From another direction, Tony walks into the room, wearing a jovial smile.

"Agent Johnson, welcome to my humble abode. I hope you slept well. You must be hungry."

"You're delusional, Mr. Bianco."

"Oh, insults before breakfast? I don't think so. Relax. We have something to celebrate."

I can't help it, I stare at him in disbelief. Kendall could be slightly in denial about good and bad sometimes. I've met men like him before, but the true extent of their entitlement and privilege never ceases to amaze.

"I'm scared to ask," I say, not bothering with hiding the sarcasm.

"Oh, we'll definitely have to talk, but one thing at a time."

I can't help but agree. One thing has become indefinitely urgent in the past few minutes.

"Sure. I hope you don't mind if I use the restroom first?"

"Down the hall," he says, the smile still in place. "Don't try anything. It's all bolted down, you'd only hurt yourself."

Predictably, one of the goons follows, and I'm forced to leave the door ajar.

Whatever. At this point, it's not the worst thing if I don't have to pee my pants.

Bianco offers me champagne, which I decline. He pours himself a generous amount.

"What are we celebrating?"

"You really don't know? Everyone in their place. You are here, enjoying my hospitality, and the princess is behind bars. It's a good way to start the day."

"Kendall won't stay behind bars for long."

"See, that's where you're wrong. She's not going to talk. Poor thing, she got too involved. If she can keep you alive, she will."

"You're planning to keep me here indefinitely, assuming she's not going to tell on you in return? That's a big gamble." Maybe I should keep my mouth shut. As long as he thinks things are going his way, I'm enjoying a dubious sort of safety—aren't I?

"Nothing is forever, Agent Johnson, but this gives us some time."

"To do what?"

"It's better if you don't know everything." He shrugs. "Though, to be honest with you, it wouldn't make much of a difference. Enjoy the present while you can. I'd eat if I were you, and I'd have some of that champagne. It will be a very busy day for me and my family, and I'm not sure when and if someone will have time to check in on you."

"You expect me to eat like this?" I raise my bound hands.

"Are you hungry enough?"

Of course, this was merely an attempt to humiliate me. I am hungry. Asshole.

"I guess then you and your men aren't brave enough even with all those guns on you...if you're afraid of an unarmed woman with a glass of champagne?"

The smile is back in place, but I've seen the flash of anger.

"You know what, you're right." He waves one of the goons over, who cuts the ties with a knife. "Let's be polite, shall we?"

"I won't stab you with a fork, you won't shoot me in the back?"

The reference to the way Lorenzo Mancini died wasn't accidental, and I'm sure Tony didn't understand it as such.

He chuckles. "Works for me. Let's eat."

Various thoughts are chasing one another in my head, scenarios in which I could make it out of here. Hot coffee—whatever I could do with it other than drink it wouldn't do more than distract one of them for a few seconds. Enough for me to get a gun? Point it at

Bianco? As I eat, I watch the men from the corner of my eye. They are standing too close, their faces unreadable masks. Maybe they are tired, distracted, or pissed that I'm sitting here enjoying a lavish breakfast—but they are probably not slow. Will I have another chance after they tie my hands again?

"I thought you had questions," Bianco says.

"That sounds like a trap. The less I know, the safer, right?"

"That depends."

He isn't fazed at all by the implications of my question. I sit, tense, wondering if I should be more afraid. There must be a chance, at some point. I can't believe it will end like this, with him getting away.

Again, I catch a quick glimpse at the men flanking the table. One of them seems bored, almost absent. The other one watches our every move though, and I'm not so naïve to assume Tony isn't armed.

"On what? I understand you and the Mancinis go way back. Competing in business, a little personal affront here and there, but basically you try to stay under the radar of law enforcement. Killing an FBI agent isn't under the radar, Tony. They're going to come down on you hard."

He pours another glass for himself and pushes mine towards me.

"Tell me, Agent Johnson, does it look to you like I'm worried?"

I don't answer.

"That's right, I'm not. Things are under control. Kendall needs to learn a lesson. Neither her parents nor Jimmy were able to get that done, so..." He gives an exaggerated sigh. "It's up to me to do what needs to be done."

I hold his gaze despite the cold hard stare.

"I don't plan on killing you. I want her to beg like her father did."

"Why do you hate them this much?"

"I thought you did your homework," he says and finishes his glass. He refills it right away. "Mancini humiliated me, my son, our whole family. I was never going to let him get away with it. Bruno's obsession with the princess worked in my favor—that, and the fact that he isn't very smart."

"Won't he be a loose cannon when he realizes you don't have his back?"

Bianco laughs. "It's a good thing he hasn't realized that yet. Come on, have a drink. We might be here for a while."

"And where is that?"

"Like you said earlier—the less you know, the safer for you. Now don't insult me." Bianco is still smiling, but something in his tone changed. I pick up the glass.

As long as we're talking, there's hope.

Chapter Thirty

B y the time I'm able to plead my case, there's still no news from Robyn. No one is telling me anything, or they don't know either. Bail is set at a ridiculous sum, but it means I can go home. I never thought this day would come. I would have hoped to see at least some family in the courtroom, but there's no one. Of course, they have a funeral to prepare, and there's still the business, the Mancini Group, the Adria restaurants, and *Catania*.

I would cry again, but there's no time. At home, I take a quick hot shower and change into a suit. I can't leave, but that's not the point. I need the feel and look of my clothes, of a person who's in control. In charge. As for now, I still am. I spend a couple of hours on the phone with various chief officers, assuring myself that they are holding the fort.

The last call is to *Catania* to order in. While I wait for the delivery to arrive, I open a bottle of Chianti and pour myself a glass almost to the rim.

The guilt is eating at me. Why did Agent McKay think I could help him? The Biancos and my family weren't exactly close—why would I know of other homes and real estate? I hate feeling useless, but I'm about to keel over. I pick up my glass and go to my home office where I power up the computer. The folders I gave to the FBI held printouts, but I still have the original files.

What they could do with it, or what I could do with them now...I have no freaking clue. I can't leave my home. I can't do anything to help her.

My pity party is interrupted by the arrival of the food. I buzz the delivery man up, stunned when I realize he is not alone.

"Hi, Kendall," Claudia says. "I'm so glad you're home. I'm sorry I couldn't be there earlier, but we all have a lot on our plate now."

"I figured."

"Can I come in?"

"If you don't mind that I need food right now? I haven't eaten all day."

That's not entirely true. MacKenzie brought me a vending machine coffee and a granola bar, because she was afraid I might faint. It's not important.

"Sure, you go right ahead."

"Do you want anything?"

"No, thank you. I had dinner with Luca, Marc and Elena earlier."

"You have a lot to talk about," I ascertain.

"True. I'll have a glass though if you don't mind."

I take another glass out of the cabinet, and a plate for me. Claudia is wearing a black dress, black pumps. I was in her shoes not so long ago.

"I'm really sorry about Lorenzo."

"Thank you." She swallows hard. "We had our differences, but it's...hard. You know that better than anyone else." It wouldn't be a good moment to remind her that Dad and his brother Lorenzo were polar opposites.

The memory of my conversation with Robyn's dad springs to mind. He wanted to come clean.

"We'll get through this."

"Yes, about that. I assume you had some thoughts about the future."

I'm not sure whether to laugh or cry, so I do neither. "To be honest, not a whole lot of them. This morning, Bianco sent a dead rat to my cell, and then I had to prepare for my bail hearing."

I see her flinch at the mention of the rat.

"Why would he do that?"

"Agent Johnson is missing. He wants to silence me, and he thinks that is the way to do it."

"Is it?" she asks. "You know that he probably killed her already."

I stare down at my plate, no longer hungry. I hate her for pointing out the obvious—or at least, the likely.

"No. No, I don't think he'll do that as long as he thinks he can still get to me."

"She betrayed you."

"She certainly did, but I still don't want things to go down this way."

Claudia sighs. I wait, but she doesn't say anything.

"Am I supposed to guess what's on your mind?"

"Kendall...I'm really sorry. You don't want to hear this, especially now, but your actions have put all of us at risk. Whatever it is you were planning to do, I hope you can still back out of it. Not for Tony, of course, but for us. We've been through enough."

She's right, I don't want to hear this, and I don't think it's entirely fair, but it looks like I don't have a choice. There I thought the homophobia that some men in the family proudly displayed was my only problem. No one has put in the hours I have to keep the Group, Adria, and *Catania* up and running. Not Lorenzo, Luca, Marc or Claudia—but it seems like they all feel entitled to their opinion, and more.

"What's your conclusion?"

Her gaze is apologetic. "We think that for the sake of the business, to maintain trust in partners and investors, you should probably step away for a bit. It's been a lot, with your parents, and now Jimmy..."

"My parents were murdered. Jimmy is a traitor," I say sharply. "Please, don't compare them."

"I wasn't. We're just trying to do right by the business now that the generation before us is...mostly gone."

"I have always done right by the business, and I'll continue to do so. My lawyers are still negotiating on my behalf in case you were worried."

"Our lawyers," she reminds me. "The sooner we can clear this all up, the better, but in the meantime, let us help."

Help, she's calling it. That's...rich, and also smart.

"I agree that we'll have to work together. When you're ready to do that, let's have a meeting right here, and we can figure out the details. Now, if you don't mind, I've had a really long day."

"Whatever you say, Kendall. Let's have this meeting soon. A lot depends on us making the right decisions."

"Doesn't it always?" I get up to see her to the door, a not-so-subtle display that the conversation is over. "Good night, Claudia."

"Good night."

When she's gone, I return to my plate and wine, finishing both in a haze of guilt. Everything is upside down. Do I believe Blake? He seemed serious. If my father wanted to cooperate, what did that mean for the rest of us? To whom do I owe my loyalty now?

I consider calling the FBI and asking for McKay, though I'm sure my lawyer wouldn't recommend it—and besides, he won't give me any information.

I make another call, though not to McKay. I desperately need another perspective.

⸺ꝓꝓ⸺

The open bottle of wine is still on the table. She accepts when I offer her a glass.

"I thought I'd be the last person you wanted to see today," Sofia says ruefully.

We've retreated to the living area, the city in lights laid out underneath us. I can't help thinking back to when Robyn was here...Jess. When we were able to ignore the looming chasm between us, betrayal, crime, the danger to come.

"In fact, you're one of the very few people I feel I need to talk to. While I was locked up, Tony had Agent Johnson abducted."

I see her eyes widen and realize this is news to her. Sofia lives a fairly quiet and remote life under the protection of my family.

"Are you sure?"

"As sure as I am that he sent me a dead rat this morning."

She pales at that. "I'm so sorry...but again, you really think he's behind all this? What would he gain?"

"We've all learned some new information in the past forty-eight hours. Jimmy teamed up with Tony to get to my father. For several reasons, but one is that Dad had some things on him that are now in the hands of the FBI. He thinks he can still stop all of this."

"Oh yes, he surely thinks of himself as untouchable," she says bitterly. "You're not going to retract anything?"

"Frankly? I don't know what to do. My lawyer tells me that we still have a good chance, the more we give them on Tony. You know him better. Will he keep the bargain?"

"I haven't talked to Tony in a long time. Since he all but spit in my face because I tried to divorce his son." Her tone is matter of fact. I'm nearly sick with anger.

"Thank God you got away from them eventually."

"I have your parents to thank for that, and you for upholding the deal, though everyone will always associate me with that name."

"Why didn't you change it?" I ask, curious.

"My husband never agreed to a divorce. Technically, I'm still married."

I let that sink in for a moment. This is the kind of men Jimmy was sneaking around with while he was sitting at my family's table. Unbelievable.

"It's been a long time coming. They all need to go away. And for that, I need your help."

"I'm not sure what I can do, but...anything you need."

"Good. Let's bring this to an end, once and for all."

It might be the wine talking, but I'm hopeful. Tony Bianco plans for the long-term. Marina Fiori, Lorenzo Mancini, the attempt on me, all of those were quickly executed actions. He doesn't spend resources on abduction just for another murder.

We still have a chance.

Chapter
Thirty-One

T he man who walks in, interrupting the dubious peace, looks familiar. I realize who he is a split-second before Tony tells him, "Frank, sit down with us. You haven't met my guest, Agent Johnson? Agent Johnson, my son Frank."

He gives me a quick, irritated look. I nearly scoff. It's not like I am here by choice. He's the son who married Sofia Rossi and then abused her to the point she sought and found shelter with the #1 rival family. Funny how the worst in the world always comes down to the ego of some men, who just can't let it go, can't admit failure.

"We need to talk," Bianco junior says. "Right now."

"Is there a problem? I was at the office this morning. No one knows we're here."

Frank leans in to whisper something to him. In a louder tone of voice, he adds, "Just for precautions. We don't know what Bruno's going to do."

"Let me worry about Bruno. He's nobody." Tony directs his attention back at me. "It's been nice, Agent, but I'm afraid I don't have any more time to chat. I have some business to attend to." He nods to the goons, and a moment later I'm facedown, nearly in my plate as they tie my hands again. Damn it. I can only hope that time is on my side—or come up with a genius idea.

⸺ℓℓ⸺

They haul me back down the stairs and into the room I previously occupied, predictably not caring if I get banged up any more in the process. Tony must be delusional. Does he really think because of me, Kendall will give up any advantage she might have by cooperating with the authorities?

Another question springs to mind. Is it a coincidence that Frank is here? I think about how Tony talked about Al Mancini's actions, and how he's obviously still angry. Do they think Sofia might come back? Talk about delusional. What about me? Am I delusional for thinking I could still survive this?

In the daylight, and without the blindfold they haven't bothered with, I can see there's nothing in this room that could help me, nothing that could be used as a weapon. The ties are a little looser, so with some acrobatics, I manage to bring my hands back in front of me.

The door has an old-fashioned lock. I won't get anywhere without a key, and besides, they don't teach you to be MacGyver at Quantico. I'm not ready to admit that all I can do is wait—for the cavalry, or a killer.

Letting out a string of curses doesn't do much to make me feel better.

I jump back from the door when I hear the sound of the key.

Looks like I need a good idea, fast.

Chapter Thirty-Two

Tony, his son Frank, Sofia, Jimmy. There's a connection somewhere, something we haven't looked at yet. When Sofia came to live with my parents, and then moved into her own place that they provided, she came with nothing.

"Your parents never made me feel like I had to give them something in return," she recalls. "But I wanted to. I didn't have much power or access, but I was listening. I was quiet...almost invisible to the men. That's how I could provide much of the information Al had on Tony."

It takes me a few seconds to understand the implications, and they are mind-blowing.

"You knew that the FBI was going to move in that night, at the raid."

"Yes. It was going to look like a normal arrest, so Alphonso would be free to work with the FBI, without any repercussions. Of course, it didn't turn out that way." She shakes her head. "After all these years, he still wants to get back at me? The sad thing is I wouldn't be surprised. He'll stop at nothing when he thinks people need to get out of the way, but most of all he likes to see them suffer."

I can't help shuddering at her words. Getting up, I look over her shoulder and at the notes I had her write down, in the hope that it would jog something, anything.

"Would he take her across state lines?"

"I'm not sure. He knows he was already under scrutiny."

"And Frank? He's more under the radar."

She has written the location of three properties in the area that are in Frank's name. There are many more that belong to Tony, and other family members, here and across state lines. They took her at night, which gave them a head start.

"I don't know if he's that sentimental, but—" Sofia bites her lip.

"What is it?"

"It might be too far, but then again, we don't know the exact time. If they drove most of the night..." She points to one of the addresses. "This is the property Tony gave to Frank for our wedding. We didn't get married there, but it was supposed to be a getaway place...Remote. Romantic." She wraps her arms around herself, looking like she's as sick to her stomach as I am. I don't need any more explanations.

"That's got to be it. The asshole likes his metaphors."

"What are you going to do?"

That stops me in my tracks for a second, as I'm still wearing the ankle bracelet. My phone rings, the perfect excuse to stall.

"Hello."

"My princess," a drunk Jimmy Bruno slurs. Of all people...But this might be good, right? I can't lose him now. He might lead us to Bianco. Tony and his abusive loser of a son.

"Jimmy, what do you want? Where are you?"

I can see the alarm in Sofia's face. She must have been walking through a minefield of triggers lately.

"Oh, we're talking again. How lovely."

"Yes, we're talking, because apparently there's a lot you forgot to tell me." I can't let my anger get the better of me. Robyn deserves better. Sofia does too. "Let's cut to the chase. If you know where Tony is holding Agent Johnson, you need to tell me right now. You need to notify the FBI."

He has the audacity to laugh.

"And how did that work out for Al?"

My fingers form a fist, fingernails cutting into my palm. "We're not talking about that right now." Though, make no mistake, sometime soon, we will. "It's Tony they want. And they want their agent back alive."

"What if I could help with that?" he asks, sounding surprisingly sober.

"Is it the honeymoon property? The one Tony gave Frank for his wedding with Sofia?"

"No, come on, you know it can't be that easy. You owe me, Kendall."

I don't know in which universe anyone could come to that conclusion, but I let him ramble.

"I want to see you. Alone. No funny business."

"Or this is a trap, and you have no idea where Agent Johnson is. Why should I trust you?"

"Because I was always thinking of you first."

That's rich coming from the man who had my parents killed, stole from me and was planning a hostile takeover of the business. He and Frank are the same. And sadly, too many people indulge them. Like Tony. Like, to some extent, my father. Jimmy has a point here—wanting to do the right thing didn't turn out so well for him.

"That's so generous. I still think you're bluffing, and you have Tony or Frank listening in. They get rid of me, and Robyn, they think everyone is too scared or too busy hiding away evidence to talk..."

"I'm not stupid, Kendall. When all is said and done, I'll be the only witness. Don't you think I don't know that? I need to get out of the country, but I need your help.

You get me some cash, and then I'll tell you where your girlfriend is."

"How much cash?"

I end the call and walk straight to the safe.

"What are you doing?" Sofia asks, now sounding scared.

"I have to ask you to leave now. I'll have someone drive you, and I'll send some extra security, just to be on the safe side."

"I hate to repeat myself, but Kendall, what is it you're planning to do? You can't leave!"

I ignore her, already on the phone making the necessary arrangements.

"Don't worry about me," I tell her when I'm done. "Once you're home, just stay inside and don't let anyone in for a while."

"This is crazy," she says.

"It has been for a while. Please, leave now. We'll talk later."

I try to keep my voice low and reassuring. I'm only moderately convincing.

"You shouldn't be alone right now, and you shouldn't go anywhere near Bruno. You know what he did. You were right the first time, this is a trap!"

"Aren't you tired of all of them behaving like they're Gods, like we should cater to their every whim? I know I am. I want it to end."

"I want that too. Why don't you contact the FBI?"

"To tell them what? We have a hunch? We don't even know for sure. I promise you, I'm not going to do anything stupid. The driver is waiting for you in the lobby. Go."

She still looks worried, but to my relief, she doesn't protest.

"Call me as soon as you know anything."

"Of course. I promise."

I wait for a few minutes. The sound of the elevator signals her departure. The driver is a woman that I picked right after firing the one who conspired with Jimmy to abduct Robyn. The memory still makes me breathless with rage, though I can't dwell on the past.

It comes down to the two of them again. I don't believe for a second that he doesn't have an agenda which might or might not include Tony. I'll head back to the safe and take out the gun.

I'm aware that my actions will have consequences. I'll deal with them later. There is no choice.

When I'm ready, to go to the kitchen where I find tools to remove the ankle bracelet.

From now on, every minute counts.

Chapter Thirty-Three

I was worried about Tony, or his son being back so soon. I didn't expect Jimmy Bruno walking through that door, and I'm not convinced that this isn't worse. Remembering what happened the last time I saw him, I shrink back.

Is that the end of it? Did Tony send him to kill me?

"Jimmy, whatever you're planning to do, think carefully. You made mistakes, but you can still deliver Tony. I'm sure he had something over you."

He shakes his head, laughing. "Save it. Let's go."

"Where are we going?"

"If you don't shut up and come with me, it will be too late. We're going to meet Kendall."

"Is that so? You're lying. She was arrested yesterday."

"Look," he says, moving so far into my personal space we're almost nose to nose. "Tony tells me to take care of you. There's no one here right now, so you can either come with me, or we'll wait until he's back, and then there's no way I can protect you."

The disbelief must have shown in my face. Protect me? Talk about delusional, and patronizing.

"Don't flatter yourself," he adds. "He wants me to go down for all of it, I don't think so. Come on."

Looks like I'll have to take my chances with one criminal versus another. But this one is on his own.

~ ele ~

"What happened to Kendall? She got out?" I ask when we're in the car. He still has the gun trained on me, but he'll be driving. There's got to be an opportunity.

"Shut up," he hisses.

"As you wish."

I can smell alcohol on his breath. This doesn't bode for a smooth ride. The sooner this is over, the better. Tony and his minions took my watch and cell phone, but I'll be able to use Jimmy's. The farther we get away from that house, the better.

The sun is starting to set when he slows down about twenty minutes later and turns onto a dirt road. There's a corn field on one side.

When he brings the car to a halt, I tense, but he takes out his cell phone while still holding the gun.

"She's here with me," he says. "You have half an hour. Then I'm going with Tony's plan."

I'm afraid that half an hour will not be enough, wherever she is right now. I'll have to take matters into my own hands.

He's still on the phone, arguing. The moment he turns his attention away from me, I open the door, get out and run.

Ignoring his angry shouts, I head straight for the corn field. My hands are still bound in front of me, and I'm too slow, stumbling, making too much noise. I don't know if my senses are playing tricks on me, but the sounds of footsteps seem not only behind me but coming from a different direction.

I come to a clearing, thinking I might make it to the main road when I hear the voice behind me.

"Agent Johnson. I don't remember saying you could leave."

Tony Bianco's jovial tone turns my stomach. I didn't think he'd get here so soon.

Shit.

A heavily breathing Jimmy Bruno is breaking through the corn.

"I caught her trying to get away," he huffs. "I followed her."

"Did you?" Tony asks. "This is already irritating. Do what I told you. Let's get this over with."

"Sure."

He doesn't move, though, and there's obviously something in his tone that gives Bianco pause. I can tell he's suspicious.

"Go ahead."

"After that we're even. I don't owe you." Jimmy isn't hiding any longer. He knows that neither of us have a good chance to get out of this, even if he kills me right now.

"Isn't that what we agreed on, son?"

"You're lying to me!" Bruno yells. "I know what you're up to."

"Jimmy, don't be an idiot."

Jimmy, however, doesn't see the signs. He just keeps talking. "You were going to let me take the fall."

"Nonsense," Bianco denies, his tone mild. "You'll be fine."

Every muscle in my body tenses.

"Because you're going to pull the trigger, right?" Bianco continues. "You did it before. It's easy. See?"

I gasp when he fires the gun. It's not me, but Jimmy who staggers and falls to the ground, whimpering. Tony's patience with his henchmen, and one in particular, has come to an end.

I don't think I have any bargaining chips left. Tony raises the gun again, but he doesn't make the shot.

Someone else is faster, hitting him first. He drops the weapon.

Kendall rushes to my side. "Are you hurt?"

"Could be worse. You have a phone? How are you here? Forget about that, I'm so happy to see you."

She touches my cheek gently while keeping an eye on Jimmy who's struggling to get up. "I'm happy too. Let's clean up this mess."

Kendall hands me Jimmy's gun, which is a good thing, because it's not over yet. I see her eyes widen, look behind her where Tony Bianco has gotten his bearings. Even hurt, she manages to spin around and fire, and again until he stops moving.

He shot her. The realization chills me to the bone. For obvious reasons, and some I'm not able to admit. I steady her when she stumbles, an awkward attempt with my bound hands, and she's slipping from my grasp. I move with her to alleviate the fall.

"Kendall!"

"I'll be okay," she mumbles. "I don't regret anything."

Seeing Jimmy hobble away, I make a decision. He won't get far anyway. And I need to be with her right now, for whatever comes next.

I saved her life a few days ago. Kendall found me. She returned the favor, and it might come at a terrible cost.

"Stop talking like that," I implore as I'm trying to halt the flow of blood while using her phone to call 911. It's hard to hide my state of mind, my voice frantic.

"Don't worry about me. I'll be fine," Kendall whispers.

"Don't you dare lie to me...ever again."

The last part elicits a wry smile. "I promise."

I'll hold her to it. The sun is setting further, dark settling around us. How terribly fitting. My eyes are stinging, yet I continue my efforts.

She can't leave me. I won't let her.

Chapter Thirty-Four

I t doesn't hurt yet which I find surprising. Good drugs, most likely. For now, they take care of everything. Another surprise is the fact that there isn't a cuff on me, though I have no illusions concerning my situation. I'm sure there's an officer or two outside the door, and the hospital room isn't the posh place I would be in if this had happened before my arrest.

I struggle to remember what exactly happened, Jimmy, Tony...One is dead, the other isn't. Did they get Frank? Is Jimmy talking already?

This is all bad, but I'm sure I remember that Robyn was okay. In fact, her voice was the last thing on my mind before the lights went out. I guess the story ends here, because I didn't stick to the conditions of the house arrest. You could say I destroyed government property as well, because they won't be able to use that bracelet again.

Whatever.

I kept my promise, with some help from unusual sources—or perhaps not so unusual, considering what Dad was about to do. Would he have gone to prison? Into witness protection? All that heartache, all that killing myself to keep business and family together—I've been living on borrowed time. It's not an uplifting thought, but even so, I can't keep my eyes open any longer.

———ℓℓ———

The next time I come to, it's with the sensation of a gentle touch to my forehead.

"Jess." Blame it on the drugs, or me wishing I could turn back time to when I thought I had it all under control. I'd better see my lawyer soon. I don't do uncertainty well, and I need to know how bad the damage is.

"I'm sorry, it's me," Sofia says apologetically. Mixed in with the disappointment is relief that she's okay. Everyone has to be aware of Tony's death by now. Lorenzo, Tony, an eye for an eye, I doubt it will end here.

But I've done the job, right?

"How are you feeling?" she asks.

"Like crap."

It worries me a little that she doesn't dispute my statement. "How bad is it?"

"The lawyers will have a word to make sure they can best represent you, and they advise you not to talk to any investigator before that is done. With one exception maybe."

Sofia smiles before she squeezes my hand and leaves the room.

Robyn Johnson walks in, looking a bit worse for wear. Halfway across the room, she halts.

"I'm still mad at you," I say the first thing that springs to mind.

A smile tugs at the corners of her mouth. She looks tired, I notice. Probably not worse than me, though.

"Not that mad. You took a bullet for me."

"I guess I owed you. Now we're even."

Robyn takes a few steps closer to the bed. I catch myself wishing she could stay, if only for a few minutes. Except for Sofia, who has a lot on her own plate, I won't have many visitors besides lawyers and FBI agents. Remembering my conversation with Claudia makes me cringe. They aren't subtle. I'll have to get out of this bed as soon as possible, salvage whatever I can.

"Thank you," she says. "You came for me."

"I'm glad I could help. I'd say it was because of fond memories, but the truth is...I couldn't let them win. And I didn't want you to pay for the choices I made."

She nods, looking serious. Even worse for wear, she's...someone I would have liked to meet under different circumstances. Someone to present to the family. Come to think of it, even the family I imagined was much of a lie.

"I appreciate you didn't tell anyone...about us."

I try to shrug, then reconsider as the pain pierces the cocoon of meds.

"I can't speak for my cousins, but so far it didn't seem to make a good bargaining chip. Screwing with bail to go find you might have tipped somebody off."

"Yes. I know. Maybe I don't care."

"So, you'll come see me in prison for a conjugal visit?" This doesn't sound as sarcastic as I'd planned.

Robyn looks behind her as if to make sure the door is still closed, then she leans in and kisses my cheek.

"That's not such a bad idea."

It definitely is, but we started out on a bad idea, and we both survived. This might be the beginning of a great love story—with a little sarcasm to it.

"I'm counting on you. Don't let me down."

Perhaps I gained a friend after all. The future will tell.

About the Author

Barbara Winkes writes suspense and romance with lesbian characters at the center. She has always loved stories in which women persevere and lift each other up. Expect high drama and happy endings. Women loving women always take the lead.

barbarawinkes.wordpress.com

Acknowledgments

Dominique, for helping make Kendall and Robyn come to life and bring them from an idea all the way to the finished book. I couldn't ask for a better partner for this and any other life's adventures.

May Dawney, for working with me on the beautiful cover art, and convincing me this story should be available in more than one medium. It took me some time, but I did it.

Anne Hagan, KC Luck, and all the authors and readers at iReadIndies for being a constant source of support and inspiration, and answering questions about the pesky details.

TB Markinson and Miranda MacLeod, for providing another important resource for sapphic authors in I Heart Lesfic.

Angela Crandall, for being generous with advice and answering even more questions.

Kimberly Amato, for the conversations and encouragement.

All my readers, for making the dream come true.

Thank you so much!